BREAKING THE ETERNAL VEIL

KIEASHA DI PAOLA

MILTON & HUGO L.L.C.
4407 Park Ave., Suite 5
Union City, NJ 07087, USA

Website: *www. miltonandhugo.com*
Hotline: *1- 888-778-0033*
Email: *info@miltonandhugo.com*

Ordering Information:
Quantity sales. Special discounts are granted to corporations, associations, and other organizations. For more information on these discounts, please reach out to the publisher using the contact information provided above.

ISBN-13:   979-8-89285-738-3   [Paperback Edition]
              979-8-89285-737-6   [Digital Edition]

Rev. date: 11/12/2025

1

A WHISPER OF THE UNSEEN

Sophia Ardent tucked her psychology textbook under her arm, the crisp autumn air wrapping around her like an old friend. Her tall, athletic frame moved gracefully across the cobblestone paths of Greystone University, the muscles beneath her golden skin flexing with each step. Long, curly brown hair tumbled over her shoulders, catching the soft afternoon sunlight and framing her striking olive-hazel eyes, which scanned the Gothic architecture with quiet curiosity. Leaves crunched beneath her boots as she passed ivy-clad brick buildings, and the reflective pond near the library shimmered like liquid gold.

It was peaceful here, and yet peace felt like an elusive concept to Sophia lately.

Her dreams had been strange these past few weeks—vivid images of light, shadows, and voices she could never quite understand. Meditation, a habit she'd picked up in an effort to clear her mind, had only deepened the strangeness. Sometimes, she felt as though she were standing on the edge of a vast, unseen world, her fingertips brushing its surface.

"Lost in thought again?"

Sophia turned, startled, to find her roommate, Maddie, jogging up beside her. Maddie was a stark contrast to Sophia's introspective nature—blonde, bubbly, and perpetually late to class.

"Sorry," Sophia said, smiling. "Just…thinking."

"About what?" Maddie asked, nudging her playfully. "Midterms? Or that new yoga instructor you keep raving about?"

Sophia laughed, though her mind lingered elsewhere. "Neither. Just…dreams, I guess."

Maddie raised an eyebrow but let it drop. "Well, don't get too dreamy, or you'll be late. Professor Grayson isn't exactly known for his patience."

The two parted ways at the entrance to the psychology building, but as Sophia walked through the lecture-hall doors, she felt it again—that strange pull.

It started that morning. She'd seen him once while crossing the quad. A tall figure leaning casually against a lamppost, his striking features impossible to ignore. His face, sculpted and ancient, seemed familiar in a way that made no sense. He wasn't one of the students or professors she recognized, and yet he felt…known.

Sophia shook her head, dismissing the thought as a trick of her overactive imagination.

But then it happened again, in the library.

While searching for a book on Jungian psychology, her gaze drifted to the far end of the stacks. There he was—watching her. His eyes, an otherworldly shade of green, locked onto hers for what felt like an eternity.

Her breath caught.

But when she blinked, he was gone.

By the end of the week, Sophia could no longer ignore it. She was seeing him everywhere—outside the dining hall, near the chapel, even in her dreams.

Who was he?

And why did it feel like her world was shifting every time their eyes met?

Sophia knew one thing for certain: Whoever—or whatever—this man was, he wasn't ordinary. And for the first time in her life, she began to wonder if her fascination with the unseen wasn't entirely one-sided.

Sophia Ardent was an enigma to many. At first glance, her confident stride and striking beauty—long chestnut hair, piercing hazel eyes, and a natural elegance—drew attention effortlessly. But beyond the surface, she was an introspective, curious soul. Friends often teased her for reading ancient philosophy texts for fun or listening to lectures on metaphysics during her morning runs.

"Soph, you're like...ninety years old inside," Maddie joked one evening as they sprawled on their dorm-room floor.

"I just like to understand things," Sophia had replied, twisting a lock of hair absently. "You know, how the mind works. How the world works. How...everything fits together."

Her curiosity often veered toward the unexplainable. Over the years, she'd devoured books on dream interpretation, energy healing, and the history of mysticism. Maddie teased, but Sophia's fascination was serious. It wasn't just academic; it was personal.

Since childhood, Sophia had felt that the world around her was layered, like a painting with hidden brushstrokes beneath the surface. Shadows moved in ways they shouldn't. Whispers lingered in empty rooms. And her dreams—they were more vivid than reality, some nights.

For years, she'd suppressed those feelings, labeling them as tricks of the mind. But lately, they were harder to ignore.

A Growing Sense of the Unseen

One afternoon, during a meditation session, Sophia felt something strange.

She was sitting cross-legged by the campus pond, her hands resting on her knees, the autumn breeze rustling the leaves around her. As she focused on her breathing, she became aware of an energy—a warm, tingling sensation running through her fingertips.

Her eyes flew open.

For the briefest moment, the world looked different. The pond shimmered as though lit from within, and the golden hues of the trees seemed brighter, almost alive.

Then it was gone.

Sophia's heart raced. She closed her eyes again, trying to recapture the feeling, but it evaded her. Was it just her imagination? Or had she glimpsed something real?

That night, she dreamt of the green-eyed man again.

Sophia's Circle

Sophia wasn't exactly a loner, but she wasn't part of the campus social whirlwind either. Maddie was her closest friend, an extroverted prelaw student with a love for coffee-fueled debates and late-night karaoke.

"Okay, let's hear it," Maddie said one evening, plopping onto Sophia's bed with a bowl of popcorn. "You've been spacing out for days. What's going on?"

Sophia hesitated, unsure how to explain. "I...I've been seeing someone."

Maddie's eyes widened. "What?! Who?"

"No, not like that," Sophia said quickly. "I mean, I keep seeing this man. Around campus. In my dreams. Everywhere. But it's weird—like, no one else seems to notice him."

Maddie frowned. "Is he...following you? Should we tell someone?"

"No, it's not like that," Sophia said, shaking her head. "He doesn't feel dangerous. If anything, I feel..." She struggled for words. "Drawn to him. Like I know him somehow."

Maddie raised an eyebrow. "Okay, now you're officially creeping me out. Maybe it's stress? Or, I don't know, some hot TA you noticed, and your brain is filling in the blanks?"

Sophia laughed weakly, but the unease lingered. Deep down, she knew this wasn't just her imagination.

The First Meaningful Encounter

It happened late one evening after a study session in the library. Sophia was walking back to her dorm, the cool air tingling against her skin. The campus was nearly deserted, the only sounds the rustle of leaves and the faint hum of a distant lamppost.

She felt it before she saw him—a shift in the atmosphere, as though the air itself was charged with electricity.

And then there he was.

He stood beneath a lamppost, its golden light casting soft shadows across his chiseled features. His green eyes met hers, and she froze. This time he didn't disappear.

"Who are you?" The words escaped her before she could stop them.

He tilted his head slightly, studying her with an intensity that made her breath catch.

"You can see me," he said, his voice deep and smooth, like the sound of a distant storm.

Sophia's heart raced. "Of course, I can see you. You're standing right there."

A faint smile touched his lips, but his eyes were filled with something else—something that looked like wonder. "You shouldn't be able to."

Sophia frowned. "What does that even mean? Why do I keep seeing you everywhere? What do you want?"

He took a step closer, his presence both magnetic and overwhelming. "It's not what I want," he said quietly. "It's what you are becoming."

"What I'm…becoming?" she echoed, her voice trembling.

Before he could answer, the faint sound of footsteps echoed in the distance. Zephyriel's head snapped toward the sound, his expression darkening. "I can't stay," he said, his voice low. "But you need to be careful, Sophia. There are things in this world—things beyond your understanding. And they're watching you now."

Her stomach knotted. "Wait—"

But before she could say more, he turned and walked into the shadows, vanishing as though he had never been there.

Sophia stood there for what felt like an eternity, her mind spinning with questions.

Who was he?

And what was she becoming?

Chapter

2

AWAKENING

Sophia barely slept that night.

The stranger's words—*what you are becoming*—echoed in her mind, mingling with the memory of his impossibly green eyes. She'd read enough about spiritual phenomena to know that some things defied logic, but this...this felt too real, too specific.

By morning, her resolve was set. She couldn't ignore this any longer. If something was happening to her, she needed answers.

A New Sense of Power

The next few days passed in a haze of heightened awareness. Sophia began to notice things she'd never paid attention to before.

In the quiet of her dorm room, she sensed faint ripples in the air, as though invisible threads connected everything around her. On the quad, she noticed birds moving in synchronized patterns that felt deliberate. Even Maddie's energy seemed brighter, her laughter carrying a warmth Sophia could almost feel on her skin.

One afternoon, while sitting by the pond, she decided to test her instincts.

Closing her eyes, she focused on her breathing, just as Zephyriel had appeared when she meditated. The world around her faded, replaced by a soft hum—low and rhythmic, like the heartbeat of the Earth itself.

She stretched out her hand, letting her fingers hover over the water. The tingling sensation returned, stronger this time, like static electricity dancing across her skin. Slowly, the water beneath her palm began to ripple, as though responding to her presence.

Sophia gasped and jerked her hand back, the ripples vanishing instantly.

"Okay," she whispered to herself. "This is definitely not normal."

Research and Reflection

Sophia spent hours in the library, devouring books on spirituality, angelology, and metaphysics. She pored over texts about energy fields, sacred geometry, and the concept of higher planes of existence.

But none of it explained *him*.

Zephyriel.

The name had imprinted itself on her mind, though he'd never spoken it. She wasn't sure how she knew it—only that it felt right, as though it had always been there, waiting for her to remember.

Her research uncovered myths about guardian spirits and celestial beings tasked with guiding humans. But nothing she read explained why she could see him or why he seemed so protective of her.

The Second Encounter

It was late one evening, and Sophia was walking back from the campus coffee shop with Maddie. The night was cool and quiet, the stars sharp against the dark sky.

"So, are we finally admitting this mystery guy is a ghost or something?" Maddie teased, sipping her latte.

Sophia rolled her eyes. "He's not a ghost. I don't know *what* he is, but—"

She stopped mid-sentence, her gaze locking onto a figure standing beneath the old oak tree at the edge of the quad.

It was him.

Zephyriel stepped forward, his presence undeniable. Dressed simply in dark jeans and a gray coat, he looked like any other student—except for his piercing green eyes, which seemed to glow faintly in the moonlight.

Maddie followed Sophia's gaze and frowned. "Who's that?"

Sophia hesitated. "You…can see him?"

"Uh, yeah?" Maddie said, confused. "Do you know him?"

Sophia's heart raced. This was new. No one else had ever acknowledged him before. "Wait here," she said, handing Maddie her coffee.

She approached him slowly, her voice low. "You're back."

"I never left," Zephyriel said, his tone soft but firm.

Sophia glanced over her shoulder at Maddie, who was watching them with open curiosity. "She can see you. Why?"

"I've taken a form they can perceive," Zephyriel explained, his gaze flickering toward Maddie before returning to Sophia. "But that's not what's important."

"Then what is?"

Zephyriel stepped closer, the air between them charged. "You're awakening faster than I expected. Your powers—they're drawing attention. Dangerous attention."

Sophia swallowed hard. "What does that mean?"

"It means you're not safe here," he said, his voice laced with urgency. "The Council has noticed you. And if they think you're a threat, they won't hesitate to intervene."

"The Council?"

Zephyriel hesitated, glancing around as though sensing unseen eyes. "The ruling body of the celestial order. They enforce the laws of our kind. And they don't look kindly on humans who cross the boundaries."

Sophia's chest tightened. "What boundaries? I haven't done anything."

"You exist," Zephyriel said simply. "And that's enough."

A Warning Delivered

Zephyriel's gaze softened, and he reached out, his hand hovering near hers. "You need to trust me, Sophia. Things are about to get much harder for you, and I can't always protect you."

Her pulse quickened at the intensity of his words, the weight of his presence. "Why me?" she whispered. "Why is this happening?"

He hesitated, his green eyes searching hers. "Because you're not like them. You never have been."

Before she could press him for answers, a sharp gust of wind swept through the quad, scattering leaves and breaking the moment.

Zephyriel's expression hardened. "They're watching. I have to go."

"Wait—"

But he was already gone, dissolving into the shadows as though he had never been there.

Sophia stood rooted to the spot, her mind a storm of questions.

Behind her, Maddie called out, "Soph? What's going on? Who *was* that?"

Sophia turned, forcing a weak smile. "Just...someone I needed to talk to."

But deep down, she knew this was only the beginning.

The Next Days

Sophia couldn't stop thinking about him. Every time she closed her eyes, the memory of those green eyes—piercing, knowing, impossible—stayed with her. She tried to focus on classes, on Maddie's chatter, on the mundane motions of life; but her thoughts kept drifting back to the strange, impossible man who seemed tethered to her fate.

And then she started seeing him again.

It began subtly at first: a flash of movement out of the corner of her eye while walking to class, a ripple of presence near the library entrance. She caught herself staring at empty hallways, heart fluttering, convinced she'd glimpsed him again.

"Okay, that's...definitely creepy," Maddie said one afternoon as Sophia paused mid-step, her gaze locked on an empty hallway. "Unless you're inventing ghost friends now. Which, I mean... wouldn't be the weirdest thing about you."

"I'm not inventing him," Sophia said firmly. Her voice betrayed none of the rapid thrum in her chest. "I know what I saw. I feel him."

Maddie raised an eyebrow. "Uh-huh. Mr. Mysterious Man. Sure, Soph."

Sophia rolled her eyes but allowed herself a small smile. "Yes, him. And...I can't stop thinking about him."

Maddie gave a knowing grin. "Ah, the curiosity/desire cocktail. Dangerous combo. Do I need to get the first-aid kit?"

"Very funny," Sophia said, though a faint blush tinged her cheeks.

The Pond

Later that evening, Sophia returned to the pond—the one where her powers first awakened. She had a strange feeling in her chest, a mix of dread and longing, as if the air itself whispered secrets she was only half ready to hear.

She sat on the edge, letting her fingers hover above the water. The surface rippled, as if acknowledging her presence. And then there he was.

Zephyriel. Standing across the pond, illuminated by the pale moonlight. He didn't step closer, didn't speak at first. He simply watched.

Sophia's pulse leapt. "You're...here again," she said softly, though not really expecting an answer.

"I told you, I never left," he said, voice barely above a whisper, carrying across the water with the wind.

She swallowed, curiosity mingling with something she couldn't name. "Why now? Why do you...appear and vanish like this?"

Zephyriel tilted his head slightly, green eyes gleaming like sunlight through leaves. "Because you need to see. To learn. And perhaps... because you need to feel."

Sophia's heart stuttered. She frowned, quirking one eyebrow in her habitual manner, a nervous tic when she was thinking too hard. "Feel what?"

"You'll understand soon," he said, though the hint of a smile tugged at the corners of his mouth. "But it's not yet time for everything to be revealed."

She studied him, daring to step a little closer. "I hate waiting."

"You will learn," he said softly. Then almost teasingly, he said, "But waiting has its lessons too."

Sophia frowned. "I'm not exactly the patient type."

"You will be," he murmured. And for a moment, his voice held a weight that made her stomach tighten with both anticipation and unease.

The Library

The next day, Sophia found herself at the library again, her notes scattered across the table, books open on angelology, celestial lore, and metaphysical phenomena. She scribbled furiously, trying to make sense of the chaos in her mind.

And then she felt it—a familiar pull at the edge of her awareness, a warmth that made her pulse race. She looked up.

There he was. Zephyriel. Leaning against a stack of books, not quite hiding, not quite revealed.

"Back again," she whispered, barely audible.

"I told you, I never left," he said, softer this time, closer.

The distance between them seemed measured, deliberate, charged.

Sophia bit her lip, curiosity burning. "You...watch me?"

"Only when necessary," he replied, green eyes glinting with amusement—or was it mischief? She couldn't tell.

She tilted her head, quirking her signature eyebrow. "And...are you necessary right now, or just...nosy?"

He didn't answer immediately. He only watched, an unreadable expression on his face that made her pulse race in ways she didn't fully understand.

"You're...frustrating," she said, half-chiding, half-admiring.

"That is part of the awakening," he murmured.

Sophia blinked. "Frustration as a spiritual lesson?"

"Yes," he said simply. Then his tone shifted, serious and low. "And protection. You are becoming...more than you know. And that will draw those who wish to harm you."

She felt a chill run down her spine, despite the warmth of his presence. "I...can I...rely on you?"

His gaze softened for just a fraction of a second, a flicker of vulnerability passing through his expression. "I am here. Always. But there are limits, Sophia. Limits I cannot cross—not yet."

The ache of not knowing, the pull of desire, the fear of danger—all mingled inside her. And yet she felt braver than ever.

"I'll figure it out," she said, voice low, determined. "I always do."

Zephyriel studied her for a long moment, green eyes unreadable. Then, without a word, he stepped back, blending with the shadows of the stacks, disappearing before she could reach him.

Sophia exhaled, leaning back in her chair. Her fingers twitched as if remembering his touch. She felt alive, scared, and drawn to him all at once.

Maddie's voice buzzed in her mind, teasing: *Did you just get ghost-stared again, or is this a new level of weird?*

Sophia smiled faintly. "Both," she whispered, though her heart beat fast. She couldn't shake the pull of him, of what he was, of the mysteries surrounding him—and of the danger that seemed to follow whenever he appeared.

And as she stared at the empty space he had occupied, she felt it—a soft vibration, a promise, a whisper in the shadows: He would reveal himself...eventually.

But not yet.

Chapter

3

THREADS OF FATE

The Revelation

The moment came late one night. Sophia had been dreaming of Zephyriel again, but this time, it wasn't the usual strange flashes of light or vague sensations. This dream felt real.

In it, she was a child again, no more than six, running through a sunlit meadow. Behind her, a tall figure followed, his presence both protective and distant. She couldn't see his face, but she felt safe, as though no harm could reach her while he was near.

When she woke, her heart was racing.

She sat up in bed, the dream's vividness lingering like the scent of rain. It wasn't until she turned her head that she saw him, sitting in the corner of her room, his green eyes glowing faintly in the moonlight.

"Zephyriel?" she whispered, clutching the blanket to her chest.

"I didn't mean to wake you," he said, his voice low and calm.

"You're here," she said, her voice trembling. "Why are you here?"

He stood and crossed the room, his movements fluid and deliberate. "Because it's time you knew the truth."

Sophia's breath caught. "The truth about what?"

Zephyriel hesitated, his gaze searching hers. "About who I am. About why you can see me."

The air in the room seemed to hum, and Sophia felt a shiver run down her spine. "Tell me," she said, her voice steadier than she expected.

He exhaled slowly, as if bracing himself. "Sophia, I am your guardian angel. I've been watching over you since the moment you took your first breath."

Her eyes widened. "What?"

"It's my purpose," he continued. "My duty. Every soul is assigned a guardian, a protector to guide them and keep them safe. For years, I've been by your side, unseen, unheard. Until now."

"Why now?" she asked, her voice barely a whisper.

"Because you're different," Zephyriel said, his green eyes glowing brighter. "Your soul isn't like others. You've always had a connection to the spiritual world, but now, it's awakening. You're beginning to see the things most humans never could—including me."

Sophia stared at him, her mind spinning. "All this time...you've been there? Watching me?"

"Yes," he said, his voice softening. "I've seen you laugh. I've seen you cry. I've seen you face pain and fear and doubt, and every moment, I've been there, shielding you from what I could."

A memory surfaced—an image of a car accident she had narrowly avoided as a teenager, the strange sensation of being "pulled" to safety.

"That was you," she said, the realization hitting her like a wave.

He nodded.

Her emotions surged—gratitude, confusion, awe. "Why me? Why did you choose me?"

"I didn't choose," he said, his gaze unwavering. "You were entrusted to me. But..." He hesitated, the faintest trace of vulnerability crossing his face. "Over time, it became more than duty. Watching you, protecting you—it became personal."

Sophia's chest tightened. "Zephyriel..."

His name hung between them, a bridge neither dared to cross. For a moment, the only sound was the soft rustling of leaves outside her window.

Then, he spoke again, his voice filled with quiet intensity. "You're the reason I exist, Sophia. And I will protect you until my very last breath."

Threads of Fate

The revelation left Sophia reeling, but it also deepened her connection with Zephyriel. Their friendship grew stronger, built on a foundation of trust and shared understanding.

Her days were still filled with the routines of college life—classes, study sessions, and late-night talks with Maddie. But her nights were something else entirely.

Each evening, she and Zephyriel would meet in the clearing by the woods, where he taught her to channel the energy she could now sense all around her.

"Focus," he said one night as she held her hands out before her, trying to summon the golden motes of light.

"I'm trying," she said, frustration creeping into her voice. "It's not working."

"It's not about trying," Zephyriel said, stepping closer. "It's about letting go. Stop forcing it and just feel."

Sophia closed her eyes, exhaling slowly. She let her thoughts drift away, focusing instead on the warmth of the energy flowing through her.

This time, when she opened her eyes, the golden motes appeared, swirling around her like tiny fireflies.

A grin spread across her face. "I did it!"

Zephyriel's lips quirked into a rare smile. "Yes, you did."

Their eyes met, and for a moment, the world seemed to stand still. Sophia felt a warmth spread through her chest, different from the energy she had summoned—deeper, more intimate.

"Thank you," she said softly.

"For what?"

"For everything. For being here. For…caring."

Zephyriel's expression softened. "You don't need to thank me, Sophia. It's my greatest honor."

The words hung in the air, heavy with meaning.

A Shared Moment

One night, after a particularly challenging training session, they sat together by the pond, the moonlight casting silvery reflections on the water.

"Do you ever wish you could be...normal?" Sophia asked, staring at the rippling surface.

Zephyriel glanced at her, his expression thoughtful. "What do you mean by normal?"

"Human," she said. "Living a regular life. Not being bound by all these rules and...responsibilities."

He was silent for a moment. "There are times," he admitted. "But then I remember that my purpose gives me meaning. Without it, I wouldn't be who I am."

Sophia turned to him, her gaze searching his. "And who are you?"

He smiled faintly, the kind of smile that carried centuries of wisdom and sadness. "I'm someone who has found more joy and pain in these past weeks with you than in all the years before."

Her breath caught at the raw honesty in his voice.

"Zephyriel..." she began, but he interrupted her.

"You don't need to say anything," he said gently. "Just...let this moment be."

And for the first time in her life, Sophia felt truly at peace.

Building a Bond

It started with small things.

One evening, as Sophia studied in the library, she felt the familiar shift in the air that signaled Zephyriel's arrival. She didn't need to look up to know he was there; his presence was a steady warmth at her side.

"You study too much," he said, his voice low enough that only she could hear.

Sophia glanced up, suppressing a smile. "I'm trying to pass my exams. Not all of us have eternity to figure things out."

Zephyriel tilted his head, a ghost of a smile on his lips. "You're already learning more than you realize."

They fell into an easy rhythm after that. Zephyriel would show up unexpectedly—sometimes to sit with her in silence as she worked, other times to ask her questions about her classes or her life. He seemed genuinely curious about the mundane details of her existence, which struck Sophia as oddly endearing.

"You don't get bored?" she asked one afternoon as they sat by the pond.

"Of you?" he said, his green eyes meeting hers. "Never."

Her cheeks flushed, and she quickly looked away, pretending to focus on the pages of her notebook.

Navigating Two Worlds

Sophia's days were a balancing act.

By day, she attended classes, studied with Maddie, and tried to maintain the semblance of a normal college life. But her nights—and increasingly, her thoughts—belonged to Zephyriel.

Maddie noticed the change.

"You've been glowing lately," she said one morning over coffee.

Sophia nearly choked on her latte. "What?"

"You know, glowing. Like you're into someone. So who is he?" Maddie leaned forward, her eyes sparkling with curiosity.

Sophia hesitated. "It's...complicated."

"Complicated is college code for 'hot and mysterious,'" Maddie said with a grin. "Spill."

Sophia deflected, offering a vague story about a guy she'd met in one of her meditation groups. But deep down, she knew she couldn't explain Zephyriel to anyone—not without sounding completely insane.

Training Begins

One evening, after a particularly strange dream involving swirling light and a voice calling her name, Sophia found Zephyriel waiting for her outside her dorm.

"You're ready," he said without preamble.

"For what?" she asked, clutching her sweater against the cool night air.

"To learn."

He led her to the edge of campus, where a quiet clearing in the woods offered privacy. The moonlight filtered through the trees, casting everything in a soft silver glow.

"Close your eyes," Zephyriel instructed.

Sophia hesitated but complied, her heart pounding.

"Feel the energy around you," he said, his voice steady and calming. "It's always there, even if you can't see it. Breathe deeply and let yourself sense it."

At first, there was nothing. But then, gradually, she became aware of a faint hum—a vibration that seemed to pulse in rhythm with her heartbeat.

"Good," Zephyriel said. "Now focus. Imagine the energy flowing through you, like a river."

Sophia did as he said, and suddenly, the air around her shifted. The hum grew louder, and she felt a tingling warmth spread through her body. When she opened her eyes, tiny motes of golden light danced in the air around her fingers.

She gasped. "Am I doing this?"

Zephyriel nodded, his expression unreadable. "You're capable of more than you know."

Growing Closer

As their training sessions continued, Sophia and Zephyriel grew more comfortable with each other. He began to share pieces of his own story—how he had watched over her since she was a child, how he had once believed his role was purely protective.

"But then you started to change," he admitted one night as they sat by the pond. "You began to sense things no human should. And I realized…you weren't like the others I've guarded."

Sophia looked at him, her chest tightening. "What does that mean?"

"It means," he said, his voice soft, "that you're extraordinary."

The intensity of his gaze made her heart race, and for a moment, she forgot to breathe.

"Zephyriel…" she began, but the words caught in her throat.
"Yes?"

She hesitated, unsure how to articulate the feelings swirling inside her. Instead, she looked away, her cheeks warm.

4

AWAKENING GIFTS

Why Train?

Sophia hadn't understood the gravity of her situation at first. When Zephyriel revealed he was her guardian angel, she'd assumed their connection was a beautiful mystery, something extraordinary but manageable. She was wrong.

"You're not just awakening to the spiritual world," Zephyriel explained one evening as they walked through the quiet woods. "You're becoming a part of it. That's why we need to train."

Sophia frowned. "Becoming a part of it? What does that even mean?"

"Your gifts are God-given," he said, his tone reverent. "You were born with the ability to sense and manipulate spiritual energy, but only now is that power beginning to manifest. Without guidance, it could consume you—or attract those who would seek to exploit it."

"Like the Council?" she asked hesitantly.

Zephyriel's expression darkened. "Among others."

He stopped walking and turned to face her, his green eyes intense. "Sophia, there are forces in Heaven and beyond that don't see your abilities as a gift. They see them as a threat to the natural order. The Council enforces the old laws, and those laws are absolute: Humans are not meant to wield celestial power."

"Then why do I have it?" she asked, her voice trembling.

"That's what we must discover," Zephyriel said. "And it's why you must learn to control your gifts. If you don't, they'll come for you."

Discovering Her Powers

Their training sessions grew more intense as Zephyriel pushed Sophia to explore the depths of her abilities.

"You can already sense energy," he said one evening, motioning for her to close her eyes. "But now, you need to learn to shape it. Focus on the air around you. Feel its movement, its weight. Now, guide it."

Sophia furrowed her brow, her hands outstretched. Slowly, she felt the air respond to her will—a gentle breeze swirling around them, growing stronger with each passing moment.

When she opened her eyes, she saw the wind bending the branches of the nearby trees.

"Did I just do that?" she asked, her voice filled with awe.

Zephyriel nodded. "Your connection to the elements is only the beginning. You're capable of much more."

Over time, Sophia discovered other abilities. She could summon light to illuminate the darkest corners of the woods. She could sense emotions in others, feeling their joy or pain as if they were her own. And with Zephyriel's guidance, she began to hone her intuition, learning to trust the whispers of the unseen world.

Zephyriel Around Her Friends

At first, Sophia worried about how Zephyriel's presence would affect her friendships. Maddie, in particular, had been curious about the mysterious man who kept showing up in Sophia's life.

"So is this guy, like, your boyfriend or what?" Maddie asked one afternoon as Zephyriel joined them for coffee.

Sophia blushed, glancing at Zephyriel. "He's…a friend."

Zephyriel smirked slightly, his expression unreadable. "You could say I'm her protector."

Maddie raised an eyebrow. "Okay, Mr. Cryptic. But seriously, what's your deal? You're like this ethereal model who just shows up out of nowhere."

"I'm just here to make sure Sophia is safe," he said simply, his tone polite but firm.

Over time, Maddie grew used to Zephyriel's presence, though she remained suspicious of his motives.

"He's got that mysterious, brooding thing going on," she told Sophia one night. "I swear, if he turns out to be a vampire or something, I'm out."

Sophia laughed, though her heart ached with the weight of the secrets she couldn't share.

The Council and the Old Laws

As their training progressed, Zephyriel began to share more about the celestial realm and its rigid hierarchy.

"The Council is the governing body of Heaven," he explained during one of their sessions. "They were created to maintain order, to ensure that the balance between the celestial and mortal worlds is never broken."

"And these old laws?" Sophia asked, summoning a small orb of light in her palm.

"They were written long ago," Zephyriel said. "The first and most important law is that angels must never interfere with the free will of humans. Our role is to guide and protect, but always from the shadows."

"But you broke that law by coming to me," she said softly, letting the light fade.

He met her gaze, unflinching. "I did. And I would do it again. Your gifts are too important to leave untended, and your life is worth more than their rules."

Sophia's heart swelled at his words, though she couldn't ignore the weight of what he'd sacrificed for her.

Deepening Their Bond

As the weeks turned into months, Sophia and Zephyriel's relationship deepened. Their shared moments during training became more personal, their conversations drifting from celestial matters to their hopes, fears, and dreams.

One evening, after an especially grueling session, they sat together on a fallen log, the stars shining brightly overhead.

"You're improving," Zephyriel said, his green eyes reflecting the starlight.

"Thanks to you," Sophia said, her voice warm.

"It's not just me," he said. "The strength was always within you. I'm just helping you find it."

Sophia looked at him, her heart pounding. "I don't know what I would've done without you, Zephyriel. You've changed my life."

He smiled faintly, his expression filled with something she couldn't quite name. "And you've changed mine."

They sat in silence for a moment, the weight of unspoken words hanging between them.

"Zephyriel," she said finally, her voice barely above a whisper. "Do you ever wish things could be different? That you could…live like we do?"

He hesitated, his gaze distant. "Sometimes," he admitted. "But my existence is tied to a higher purpose. I don't belong to this world the way you do."

"But you're here," she said, her voice firm. "With me. Doesn't that mean something?"

He turned to her, his green eyes burning with intensity. "It means everything."

Chapter

5

CROSSING THE BOUNDARY

Reading Week: Alone but Not Lonely

When reading week began, campus fell quiet as students returned home for a brief reprieve. Maddie, thrilled at the chance for home-cooked meals and family gossip, packed her bags and left without hesitation.

"Don't study too hard while I'm gone!" Maddie teased, tossing Sophia a wink as she walked out the door.

Sophia smiled, waving her off. But as soon as the door closed, a strange mixture of relief and anticipation settled over her. For the first time in months, she had the dorm—and her life—to herself.

Almost.

Zephyriel was still there, as he always was, lingering in the background like a guardian shadow. Yet lately, his presence had felt different. Closer. More tangible.

An Intimate Evening

That first evening alone, Zephyriel appeared as Sophia sat by the window, the cool night breeze brushing against her skin. She had been thinking about him, about the countless ways he had become intertwined with her life.

"You're quiet tonight," he said, his voice soft.

Sophia turned, startled. She hadn't even heard him enter. "Just thinking," she said, gesturing for him to join her.

He sat beside her, his tall frame close enough that she could feel his warmth.

"About what?" he asked.

She hesitated, her gaze drifting to the stars outside. "About you. About us."

Zephyriel's expression softened, and for a moment, he looked almost human. "And what have you decided?"

"That I don't regret any of it," she said firmly. "Even if it changes everything."

Training Takes a Turn

The next night, during a training session, the air between them seemed charged with something unspoken. Zephyriel had been teaching her to summon energy from within, to focus her will and project it outward.

"Good," he said as she formed a glowing orb of light between her hands. "Now, push it outward. Let it expand."

Sophia did as he instructed, and the light grew, radiating like a small sun. But as she held it, her focus faltered, and the orb began to waver.

"I can't hold it," she said, panic creeping into her voice.

"Yes, you can," Zephyriel said, stepping closer. "Trust yourself."

His hand covered hers, steadying her. The orb stabilized, glowing brighter. But as their hands touched, the energy shifted—warmer, more intense. Sophia felt her breath hitch, and when she looked up, Zephyriel was already watching her.

Their faces were inches apart, the light from the orb casting golden shadows across his features.

"Zephyriel…" she began, her voice barely a whisper.

He didn't move, his green eyes searching hers. "Sophia," he said softly, his voice heavy with something she couldn't name. "This isn't… what we should do."

"What if it is?" she whispered.

For a moment, time seemed to stop. The light between them flickered, then faded, leaving only the two of them in the stillness.

And then, as if drawn by an unseen force, Zephyriel closed the distance between them.

A Boundary Crossed

The kiss was unlike anything Sophia had ever known. It wasn't just physical—it was electric, a merging of energy and emotion so powerful that it felt like the world itself had shifted.

Zephyriel pulled back slightly, his expression conflicted. "This is forbidden," he said, his voice low.

"I don't care," Sophia said, her hands clutching his. "I need you."

His resolve faltered, and he kissed her again, deeper this time. The room seemed to hum with energy, the air around them charged with a light that came from nowhere and everywhere.

As their connection deepened, the celestial energy within Sophia surged, mingling with Zephyriel's own essence. It was as if their souls were entwining, forging a bond that defied the laws of Heaven and Earth.

Zephyriel kissed Sophia harder, then slowly down her neck.

Sophia moaned, and her heart raced at his touch. His large hands was running down her back and caressing her body. Sophia reached down and unbuttoned his pants.

Zephyriel watched as she did so. He then picked her up. Sophia's legs wrapped around his waist as he carried her over to the bed. He undressed her slowly, making sure to take in every moment.

Sophia felt like every touch was electric and every second an eternity. It was almost like time stood still. Sophia commented on this as Zephyriel was sliding her pants off.

"I want this moment to last forever. It feels like time has slowed down." Zephyriel looked at her with a new level of intensity and said, "That's because it has. Our connection is heightening your gifts. You are slowing down time and didn't even realize it."

Sophia's mind was spinning with lust and desire and could not quite process what he said in that moment.

She grabbed his hands and put them on her breast and pulled him closer. Zephyriel was on top of her, and she was kissing his neck all over. She looked in his green eyes, and it felt like electricity between them.

Zephryiel slipped inside her, and she gasped as all her desires were fulfilled.

The passion was unworldly as they made love in every corner of the apartment until finally it came to and end after multiple orgasms for both.

When it was over, they sat together in the golden glow of the aftermath, their breathing steadying as the energy around them calmed.

Zephyriel looked at her, his expression a mix of awe and fear. "What we've done… " he began, his voice trailing off.

"What about it?" Sophia asked, her heart pounding.

"It's more than a kiss, more than…love," he said. "We've created a bond. A celestial link that no angel is meant to share with a human. The Council will sense it."

Sophia's chest tightened. "And what will they do?"

"They'll come for you," Zephyriel said grimly. "Because now you're not just a human with powers. You're something new. Something they fear."

The Moment That Changed Everything

As the weight of his words sank in, Sophia realized the magnitude of what they had done. Their love was no longer a secret, no longer something that could be hidden in the quiet corners of the mortal world.

"What happens now?" she asked, her voice trembling.

Zephyriel took her hands, his grip firm but gentle. "Now we fight. For us. For what we've created. And for the right to choose our own destiny."

Sophia nodded, her resolve hardening. Whatever came next— whether it was the wrath of the Council or the unraveling of the heavens themselves—she would face it with him.

Together, they had crossed the boundary. And together, they would face the consequences.

Chapter

6

A STORM APPROACHES

Dreams of the Future

Sophia's dreams had always been vivid, but since she and Zephyriel had crossed the line into forbidden love, they had taken on a life of their own. No longer just scattered images or feelings, her dreams now revealed glimpses of the future—brief, fragmented visions of what might come to pass.

One night, as she slept beside Zephyriel in the quiet of her dorm room, the dream came to her like a flash of light:

She saw Maddie standing in the rain, her face streaked with tears. A choice appeared before Sophia, hazy and indistinct, but its consequences were stark. One path led to Maddie leaving her life forever, consumed by grief. The other showed Maddie safe, smiling, but at the cost of something Sophia couldn't yet understand.

Sophia woke with a gasp, her heart racing.

"What did you see?" Zephyriel asked, his voice calm but laced with concern. He sat beside her, his green eyes glowing faintly in the moonlight.

She hesitated. "A choice…for Maddie. And neither outcome feels right."

Zephyriel took her hand. "Your visions are a gift, but they're also a burden. They show possibilities, not certainties. You can still shape what comes."

"But how do I know what to choose?" she whispered.

"With time," he said softly. "And trust in yourself."

Passion Between Worlds

The days that followed were a whirlwind of passion and secrecy. The love between Sophia and Zephyriel burned like a wildfire—intense, all-consuming, and impossible to contain.

They made love wherever they could: beneath the stars in the secluded woods; in the quiet corners of Sophia's dorm room; and once, impulsively, in the empty lecture hall where Zephyriel had been waiting for her after class.

Each moment was electric, their connection deepening with every touch, every whispered promise. But it wasn't just the physical intimacy that bound them—it was the merging of their souls, the feeling of becoming something greater together than they could ever be apart.

Maddie's Suspicions

Maddie returned from reading week full of stories about her family and oblivious to the storm brewing in Sophia's life. But it didn't take long for her to notice the change in her roommate.

"You're glowing again," Maddie said one morning as she sipped her coffee. "And don't tell me it's because you aced a test. Who's the guy?"

Sophia froze mid-bite, her cheeks flushing. "What are you talking about?"

Maddie smirked. "Oh, please. I saw you two the other day in the library. You looked like you were about to devour each other."

Sophia's heart raced. "We're dating," she blurted out, hoping the lie would satisfy Maddie's curiosity.

Maddie raised an eyebrow. "Dating, huh? Well, I approve. He's ridiculously hot, and you're happier than I've ever seen you. Just don't let him distract you too much."

Sophia forced a smile, but the weight of the secret she carried felt heavier than ever.

Caught in the Act

Keeping their relationship hidden from Maddie proved more difficult than Sophia expected.

One evening, after a particularly heated training session, she and Zephyriel found themselves tangled together on her bed, their passion overriding any sense of caution.

The door burst open.

"Oh my God!" Maddie shrieked, dropping her bag. "Seriously? In our room?"

Sophia scrambled to cover herself, her face burning with embarrassment. "Maddie, I—"

"Don't even try to explain," Maddie said, backing out of the room. "Just...next time, maybe lock the door?"

When the door closed, Sophia collapsed into laughter, though her cheeks were still red.

Zephyriel chuckled beside her. "I suppose we need to be more careful."

"You think?" she teased, leaning into him.

The Classroom Incident

Sophia's newfound relationship with Zephyriel consumed her thoughts, even during class.

One day, as Professor Grayson lectured on cognitive psychology, Sophia found herself drifting into a daydream. In her mind, she replayed the memory of Zephyriel's touch, the way his green eyes seemed to see straight through her.

"Sophia!"

Her name jolted her back to reality. The entire class was staring at her, and Professor Grayson's eyebrows were raised.

"Care to share what's so fascinating?" he asked dryly.

Sophia stammered, her face hot. "Uh, sorry. I was just...thinking."

"Well, try thinking about the lecture," he said, turning back to the board.

The incident earned a few giggles from her classmates, but Sophia couldn't bring herself to care. Her mind was elsewhere—on Zephyriel, on the future, and on the storm she could feel brewing on the horizon.

Preparing for the Council

Zephyriel grew more vigilant with each passing day, his presence both a comfort and a reminder of the danger they faced.

"They'll come soon," he said one night as they trained in the woods. "The Council isn't blind to what we've done. They'll sense the bond between us, the way your powers are growing."

Sophia nodded, her jaw set. "Then we'll be ready."

"Your powers are unique," Zephyriel said, pacing as he spoke. "You're developing faster than I anticipated. Your visions are only the beginning. If you can learn to focus, you'll be able to see not just glimpses but entire paths—outcomes for yourself, for your friends, for the world."

"But what good is seeing if I can't stop what's coming?" she asked.

"That's why we train," he said. "To give you the tools to act. To change the future."

As their sessions grew more intense, Zephyriel also began teaching her about the celestial hierarchy.

"The Council isn't evil," he explained. "They believe in the laws they enforce. To them, the old ways are sacred—unchanging, immutable. But those laws were written for a different time, a different world."

"And you think they're wrong?" she asked.

"I think love isn't something that can be bound by rules," he said, his voice steady. "And I think you're proof that the world needs to change."

Sophia felt a warmth spread through her chest at his words. "You really believe that?"

"I believe in you," he said simply.

A Storm on the Horizon

Despite their training and their love, a sense of inevitability hung over them. Sophia's powers were growing stronger, her visions more vivid. But with each step forward, the shadow of the Council loomed larger.

One night, as she lay in bed beside Zephyriel, she turned to him, her voice trembling. "What if we can't stop them?"

He pulled her close, his arms strong and reassuring. "Then we face them together. Whatever comes, I won't let you face it alone."

Sophia closed her eyes, his words a balm to her fears. But deep down, she knew the time was fast approaching when they would have to fight—not just for their love, but for their very existence.

7

THE COUNCIL'S ARRIVAL

An Ominous Prelude

The air felt different that morning. Heavy. Charged.

Sophia stood at the edge of the woods where she and Zephyriel had trained for weeks, her breath visible in the crisp autumn air. Something was coming—she could feel it in her bones.

Zephyriel appeared silently at her side, his expression grim.

"They're close," he said, his green eyes scanning the horizon.

Sophia swallowed hard. "How close?"

"Hours, perhaps less," he said. "The Council doesn't send warnings. When they arrive, it's swift and absolute."

Sophia's stomach churned. She'd known this moment would come, but the reality of it was suffocating.

"Can we stop them?" she asked, her voice trembling despite her best efforts to sound brave.

"We can hold them off," Zephyriel said, turning to her. "But their power is immense. They will try to separate us—to break our bond."

Sophia met his gaze, her determination hardening. "Then we don't let them."

The Gathering Storm

The hours that followed felt like an eternity. Zephyriel guided Sophia through one final training session, pushing her harder than ever before.

"You need to stay focused," he said as she summoned a swirling orb of light. "The Council will try to manipulate your emotions. They'll use fear, doubt, even guilt to weaken you."

"I'm not afraid of them," Sophia said, though her hands shook as she held the orb steady.

Zephyriel stepped closer, his hands covering hers. "Courage isn't the absence of fear," he said softly. "It's choosing to act in spite of it. And you are the bravest person I have ever known."

Sophia looked up at him, her heart swelling with both love and fear. "Zephyriel…if this doesn't go the way we hope, I want you to know—"

He silenced her with a kiss, his lips firm and reassuring. "Don't speak of endings," he said. "We're not finished yet."

The Arrival

It happened at dusk.

Sophia and Zephyriel stood at the clearing's edge, the golden light of the setting sun casting long shadows through the trees. The air grew colder, the sky darkening unnaturally as a faint hum filled the silence.

And then they appeared.

Six figures descended from the sky, their forms cloaked in shimmering white and gold. Each radiated a presence so overwhelming that Sophia instinctively took a step back, her heart pounding.

At their center stood a tall figure with piercing silver eyes and a staff that glowed faintly in the fading light. Zephyriel's grip on Sophia's hand tightened.

"Who is that?" Sophia whispered.

"Eryon," Zephyriel said, his voice laced with tension. "The leader of the Council."

Eryon stepped forward, his gaze sweeping over the clearing before settling on Zephyriel.

"You have defied the laws of Heaven," he said, his voice reverberating like the toll of a distant bell. "And for what? This…mortal?"

Zephyriel stepped protectively in front of Sophia. "She is more than you can understand," he said firmly. "And our bond is not a crime—it's a choice."

"A choice?" Eryon's voice sharpened. "You speak of choice as though it absolves you. But you know the laws, Zephyriel. Angels do not love. Angels do not bond. And angels do not defy the Council."

Sophia found her voice, though it trembled. "Maybe your laws are wrong."

The other Council members turned their gaze on her, their combined presence nearly crushing. But she held her ground, meeting Eryon's stare.

"She is bold," Eryon said, a faint note of disdain in his voice. "But ignorance does not excuse her defiance."

"She is not ignorant," Zephyriel said, stepping closer to Sophia. "She is awakening to a power that surpasses even your understanding. And I will not let you take her."

Eryon raised his staff, the air around them shimmering with energy. "You would risk everything for this mortal? Your place in Heaven, your very existence?"

"I would," Zephyriel said without hesitation.

The Confrontation

Eryon's eyes narrowed, and in an instant, the clearing erupted in light. The other Council members raised their hands, summoning orbs of energy that crackled like lightning.

"Stay behind me!" Zephyriel shouted, pushing Sophia back as he stepped forward to meet the Council's assault.

But Sophia refused to stand idly by. Closing her eyes, she summoned the energy within her, the golden light she had practiced so many times now glowing fiercely in her hands.

When she opened her eyes, the orbs of light the Council had summoned were frozen mid-air, their energy suspended.

Eryon's gaze snapped to her, his expression unreadable. "What have you done?"

"I made a choice," Sophia said, her voice steady.

Zephyriel looked back at her, his eyes wide with a mixture of awe and pride.

"You think your fledgling power can stand against the Council?" Eryon asked, his tone both curious and disdainful.

"I think I'm done being afraid of you," Sophia said.

A Battle of Wills

The clash that followed was unlike anything Sophia had ever experienced. Zephyriel fought with a grace and ferocity that took her breath away, his every movement calculated and precise. But the Council's power was overwhelming, their attacks relentless.

Sophia focused on controlling the energy around her, deflecting blasts of light and creating shields to protect herself and Zephyriel. Her visions flashed in her mind—glimpses of possible outcomes, choices that could tip the balance in their favor.

"Zephyriel, to the left!" she shouted, seeing an attack moments before it happened.

He moved instinctively, dodging a blast of energy that would have struck him down.

"You're incredible," he said breathlessly, his gaze locking with hers for a split second before he returned to the fight.

The Aftermath

Though battered and exhausted, Sophia and Zephyriel managed to hold their ground, their combined strength forcing the Council to retreat—for now.

Eryon's parting words echoed in the clearing: "This is far from over. The laws of Heaven will not bend for love."

As the Council vanished into the night, Sophia collapsed into Zephyriel's arms, her body trembling from exhaustion.

"They'll be back," she said weakly.

"I know," Zephyriel said, his voice filled with quiet determination. "But so will we."

Chapter

8

STRENGTH IN LOVE, STRENGTH IN POWER

The Aftermath

The woods were eerily silent after the Council's departure. Sophia's chest heaved as she tried to steady her breathing, her limbs trembling from exertion. The golden glow of her summoned energy flickered out, leaving her in the dim light of the moon and stars.

Zephyriel knelt beside her, his green eyes scanning her for injuries. His touch was gentle but urgent, his hands brushing her arms and shoulders. "Are you hurt?"

"I'm fine," she said, though her voice was hoarse. "Just…drained."

He exhaled, relief softening the tension in his jaw. "You were incredible," he said quietly. "I've never seen anyone—human or angel—do what you just did."

Sophia managed a weak smile, but the weight of the confrontation lingered in her chest. "I just…reacted. I didn't even know I could do that."

"You've barely scratched the surface of your potential," Zephyriel said, his tone filled with both pride and concern. "But the Council won't underestimate you again. They'll return stronger, more determined."

Sophia looked into his eyes, the enormity of what they faced sinking in. "What if we're not ready when they come back?"

"Then we'll make sure we are," he said firmly. "We'll find a way."

Regrouping

The days that followed were a whirlwind of recovery and preparation. Zephyriel insisted on doubling their training sessions, pushing Sophia to explore the limits of her abilities.

"You've already proven you can manipulate energy and see the future," he said during one session, as she practiced forming protective shields. "But there's more. You have a connection to the spiritual realm that's unlike anything I've ever seen. You need to learn to trust it."

Sophia frowned, sweat dripping down her brow as she held the shield steady. "What does that even mean?"

"It means," Zephyriel said, stepping closer, "that your instincts are stronger than logic. When you feel something—an attack, a shift in the energy around you—you need to act without hesitation."

He raised his hand suddenly, summoning a bolt of energy that streaked toward her. Sophia gasped but didn't flinch. The shield she had created held firm, the bolt dissipating on impact.

Zephyriel smiled. "You're learning."

The Weight of Love

Though their days were consumed with training, their nights belonged to them.

The intensity of their love only deepened in the wake of the Council's attack. Each moment together felt precious, as though the world might shatter at any moment. They clung to each other in quiet desperation, finding solace in stolen kisses and whispered promises.

One evening, as they lay entwined in Sophia's bed, she traced her fingers along the contours of his face.

"Do you ever regret it?" she asked softly. "Falling in love with me? Breaking the rules for me?"

Zephyriel caught her hand, pressing a kiss to her palm. "Never," he said, his voice unwavering. "You're worth every risk, every sacrifice."

Sophia's heart swelled, but a shadow of doubt lingered. "But what if we fail? What if the Council wins?"

"Then at least we'll have this," he said, his green eyes meeting hers. "And no one can take that away from us."

Sophia's Powers Evolve

As their bond grew stronger, so did Sophia's abilities.

Her visions became more frequent, showing her not only glimpses of the future but also choices—paths that would shape the destinies of those around her.

One night, as she sat cross-legged in meditation, a vision struck her with startling clarity:

She saw Maddie standing on a crumbling bridge, her face pale with fear. A choice appeared before Sophia—save Maddie and reveal her powers to the world or let her fall and preserve the secrecy that kept her and Zephyriel hidden.

When the vision ended, Sophia's hands trembled.

"What did you see?" Zephyriel asked, sensing her unease.

"A choice," she said quietly. "And either way, someone loses."

Zephyriel knelt beside her, his hands steadying hers. "The future is fluid," he said. "Your visions show possibilities, not certainties. What matters is that you act with your heart."

Sophia nodded, though the weight of her growing abilities pressed heavily on her shoulders.

Planning for the Next Confrontation

As Sophia's powers evolved, so did Zephyriel's strategy for their survival.

"We can't rely on brute strength alone," he said one evening as they sat by the pond. "The Council's power is ancient, deeply rooted in the celestial order. But their strength is also their weakness."

Sophia tilted her head, intrigued. "What do you mean?"

"They believe in absolutes," he explained. "The old laws, the rigid hierarchy—they're inflexible. If we can show them that the world has changed, that love isn't a weakness but a strength, we might be able to challenge their authority."

"And if they don't listen?" Sophia asked.

"Then we fight," Zephyriel said, his jaw set. "But we don't fight to destroy them. We fight to show them a new way."

Sophia nodded, her resolve hardening. "Then let's make sure we're ready."

The Calm Before the Storm

Despite the looming threat of the Council's return, Sophia and Zephyriel found moments of peace amidst the chaos.

One evening, as they lay beneath the stars, Sophia turned to him, her voice soft. "Do you think we'll ever have a normal life? No running, no hiding—just us?"

Zephyriel smiled faintly, his gaze fixed on the heavens. "I don't know if normal is in the cards for us. But if there's a way, I'll find it. For you."

Sophia reached for his hand, intertwining her fingers with his. "Then I'll fight for it too."

Their bond had become unbreakable, a force that neither the Council nor the heavens themselves could severe.

But as the days passed, the weight of what lay ahead pressed heavier on their shoulders. The Council was out there, regrouping, preparing. And when they returned, Sophia and Zephyriel would face their greatest challenge yet.

Together.

Chapter

9

THE WEIGHT OF TWO WORLDS

A Balancing Act

Sophia's life was becoming a delicate juggling act. On one hand, her days were filled with the normal pressures of college—classes, study sessions, and the occasional social outing with Maddie. On the other hand, she was navigating a growing celestial power that demanded more from her with every passing day.

Her visions had become a constant presence, no longer confined to sleep. They slipped into her waking hours, flashes of what might come lingering in her mind like a half-remembered song. At first, she tried to ignore them, but they became harder to push aside.

A Family Visit

When her mother called to say she was coming to visit, Sophia felt a mix of excitement and dread.

"Sophia, sweetheart!" her mother exclaimed as they embraced on the campus quad.

Claire Ardent was the epitome of warmth, her auburn hair streaked with silver and her hazel eyes matching Sophia's. "You look so grown-up! And are those highlights in your hair? They look gorgeous."

"Just the sunlight, Mom," Sophia said with a laugh, though her mind was elsewhere.

As they walked to a nearby café, her mother chattered about life back home—how her father was struggling with the garden again, how her younger brother was excelling in soccer, and how the neighbors were asking when Sophia would visit.

"You've been so distant lately," Claire said, her tone softening as they sat down. "Is everything okay?"

Sophia hesitated, her hands tightening around her coffee cup. "I'm just…busy. College is a lot."

Her mother reached across the table, covering Sophia's hand with her own. "You can tell me anything, you know that."

Sophia swallowed hard. She wanted to confide in her mother, to share the incredible, terrifying truth of her life. But how could she explain angels and celestial councils without sounding insane?

"I'm fine, Mom. Really," she said, forcing a smile.

Claire studied her for a moment before nodding. "All right. But promise me you'll call more often. I miss my girl."

Visions of Her Friends

One evening, as Sophia walked back to her dorm, a vision struck her like a bolt of lightning.

She saw Maddie standing in a darkened parking lot, arguing with someone she couldn't identify. The argument escalated, and Maddie turned to leave—but slipped, falling hard against the pavement. A sharp pain radiated through Sophia's chest, as if she could feel the injury herself.

The vision faded, leaving Sophia breathless.

When she reached her dorm, she found Maddie sitting cross-legged on her bed, scrolling through her phone.

"Hey!" Maddie said, looking up. "You look like you just ran a marathon."

Sophia forced a laugh. "Just…stressed."

She hesitated, debating whether to say anything. The vision had felt so real, so urgent. But how could she explain it without revealing the truth?

"Maddie," she said finally, "maybe stay out of the parking lot at night. Just to be safe."

Maddie raised an eyebrow. "What's that about? Did someone creep you out?"

"No, I just…have a bad feeling," Sophia said, hoping Maddie would let it go.

Maddie shrugged. "All right, Mom. But thanks for the heads-up."

In Class

Sophia's visions began bleeding into her academic life as well.

During a lecture on developmental psychology, she found herself drifting. A flash of light filled her mind, and suddenly, she saw her professor standing in a hospital room, his face pale and filled with grief. A nurse approached him, her expression kind but firm, and Sophia heard a single phrase: *"It's too late."*

She jolted upright, her heart pounding.

"Sophia?" Professor Grayson's voice cut through her panic. "Are we keeping you awake, or would you like to contribute to the discussion?"

The class chuckled, and Sophia forced a sheepish smile. "Sorry, Professor. Just…thinking."

Grayson gave her a pointed look before continuing his lecture, but Sophia couldn't shake the image.

Confiding in Zephyriel

That night, Sophia told Zephyriel about the visions.

"They're getting more frequent," she said as they sat together by the pond. "And they're not just about me anymore. I'm seeing things—choices, events—for my friends, my professors, even strangers."

Zephyriel nodded, his expression thoughtful. "Your connection to the spiritual realm is deepening. You're not just seeing the future—you're seeing potential outcomes, paths that can be altered."

"But how do I know which ones to act on?" Sophia asked, her voice laced with frustration. "What if I make things worse?"

"Trust yourself," Zephyriel said, his hand covering hers. "Your visions are a gift, but they're also a responsibility. If something feels urgent—like Maddie's accident—act. Otherwise, observe and wait for clarity."

Sophia sighed, leaning against him. "I don't know if I'm strong enough for this."

"You are," he said firmly. "You're stronger than you realize."

A Growing Divide

Despite her efforts to maintain normalcy, the strain of her dual life began to show. Maddie noticed first.

"You've been distracted lately," Maddie said one evening as they studied together. "And I mean more than usual."

Sophia hesitated, weighing her words carefully. "I've just got a lot on my plate. Classes, personal stuff…it's overwhelming."

Maddie frowned. "You're not shutting me out, are you? Because if something's wrong, you can tell me."

Sophia smiled faintly, her heart aching. "I know. Thanks, Maddie."

But deep down, she knew there were things Maddie could never understand.

The Burden of Knowledge

Sophia's visions became increasingly vivid, each one more demanding than the last. She began to see not only potential futures but also the emotional weight of her decisions—how one choice could ripple outward, affecting countless lives.

One night, she dreamed of her father, kneeling in their family's garden with his hands in the soil. He looked peaceful, but behind him, a storm gathered on the horizon. She saw herself there, standing at a crossroads: one path led to her returning home, the other to her staying at school.

When she woke, the meaning was unclear, but the urgency lingered.

"Your visions are a tool," Zephyriel reminded her as they walked through campus the next day. "But they're not infallible. Use them to guide you, not to control you."

"I just don't want to make the wrong choice," Sophia said.

Zephyriel stopped and turned to her, his green eyes filled with quiet intensity. "The only wrong choice is doing nothing."

Preparing for What's to Come

Sophia knew that her growing powers were a double-edged sword. They gave her the ability to change the course of fate, but they also painted a target on her back. The Council would return, and when they did, she needed to be ready.

Her visions had shown her glimpses of the coming storm—blinding light, shattered ground, and a choice that would test the limits of her courage.

But for now, she focused on the present: her friends, her family, her love for Zephyriel. These were the things worth fighting for, the things that gave her strength.

As she stood at the edge of the pond, watching the moonlight ripple across the water, she made a silent promise:

She would protect the people she loved. No matter what it cost her.

Chapter

10

A GROWING LIGHT

The Depth of Her Powers

Sophia's connection to the spiritual realm was no longer just an anomaly—it was an undeniable part of her being. The visions that had once come sporadically now flowed more frequently, offering her a fragmented tapestry of possibilities.

One morning, she sat cross-legged on the dorm room floor, her eyes closed as she meditated. Zephyriel stood nearby, his green eyes watchful.

"Focus on the energy within you," he said. "It's not just a tool—it's part of who you are. Feel it, but don't try to control it. Let it guide you."

Sophia inhaled deeply, her mind sinking into a space of stillness. Slowly, she felt it: a warm, golden light glowing within her, like a flame that never extinguished. It spread through her limbs, flowing outward into the room.

When she opened her eyes, the light radiated from her hands, soft and steady.

Zephyriel smiled faintly. "You're growing stronger."

Sophia tilted her head, the light fading as her focus shifted. "But why now? Why did these powers stay dormant for so long?"

Zephyriel hesitated, as though weighing his words. "Sometimes, the soul waits for the right moment to awaken. Perhaps your bond with me was the spark you needed."

Sophia flushed, her chest tightening at the thought. "So this is because of us?"

"Partly," Zephyriel said. "But your power is your own. I'm only helping you uncover it."

A Test of Empathy

One of Sophia's most challenging powers was her ability to sense emotions. At first, it had been subtle—an awareness of people's feelings that went beyond words. But now it was overwhelming.

She felt it everywhere she went: the frustration of students cramming for exams, the quiet longing of a professor who missed their family, the bubbling excitement of friends planning a night out.

It was inescapable, and it left her emotionally raw.

"I don't know how to handle it," she confessed to Zephyriel one evening. "It's like I'm carrying everyone's feelings all the time."

"You need to learn to separate your energy from theirs," Zephyriel said. "Otherwise, it will consume you."

He guided her through an exercise, teaching her to visualize a barrier between herself and the emotions around her. At first, it was difficult— every feeling still pressed against her, insistent and unyielding. But gradually, she felt a sense of relief, like a weight lifting from her chest.

"Better?" he asked.

Sophia nodded, exhaling deeply. "Better."

Her Relationship with Maddie

Sophia's evolving powers didn't go unnoticed by Maddie, who had grown increasingly suspicious of her friend's erratic behavior.

One evening, as they sat in the dorm eating takeout, Maddie set down her chopsticks and crossed her arms.

"All right, spill. What's going on with you?"

Sophia blinked, startled. "What do you mean?"

"I mean you've been acting weird for weeks," Maddie said, her tone firm. "You're distracted, you disappear for hours, and sometimes you just...zone out completely. Are you in trouble?"

Sophia hesitated, the urge to confide in her friend warring with the need to keep her secrets. "I'm fine," she said finally. "Just…dealing with some stuff."

"Stuff," Maddie repeated, raising an eyebrow. "You know you can tell me anything, right?"

Sophia smiled faintly, her chest aching. "I know. Thanks, Maddie."

The half-truth hung between them, but Maddie seemed to accept it for now.

Visions of Love

Sophia's visions weren't always about danger or choices. Sometimes, they showed her moments of beauty and connection—like the dream she had of herself and Zephyriel walking hand-in-hand through a golden field, the sun warm on their skin.

When she told Zephyriel about it, his expression softened. "Perhaps it's a glimpse of what could be," he said. "If we survive what's coming."

Sophia touched his hand, her heart swelling with love. "We'll survive. We have to."

Strengthening Their Bond

As her powers grew, so did her bond with Zephyriel. Their connection was no longer just emotional—it was spiritual, a merging of their energies that felt as natural as breathing.

One evening, after a particularly intense training session, they sat together by the pond, the stars reflecting in the still water.

"Do you ever think about what it would be like to be human?" Sophia asked, leaning against him.

"All the time," Zephyriel admitted. "To feel the world the way you do, to live without the weight of celestial laws—it's something I'll never have."

"But you have this," she said, taking his hand. "You have us."

He looked at her, his green eyes filled with a depth of emotion that took her breath away. "And it's more than I ever thought I could have."

Their kiss was slow and deliberate, a reminder that their love was a choice they made every day, despite the risks.

A Vision of the Council

That night, as Sophia slept, a vision struck her with startling clarity.

She saw herself and Zephyriel standing in the woods, their hands clasped tightly. The Council surrounded them, their forms glowing with harsh, blinding light.

Eryon's voice echoed in her mind: "You cannot defy the laws of Heaven and expect to remain unscathed."

Sophia felt the weight of a decision pressing on her—a choice that would either save Zephyriel or doom them both.

When she woke, her body was trembling.

"What did you see?" Zephyriel asked, his voice calm but urgent.

"They're coming," she said, her voice barely above a whisper. "And this time, they won't leave without one of us."

Preparing for the Inevitable

Zephyriel took her hands, his grip steady. "Then we'll face them together. Whatever happens, we won't let them tear us apart."

Sophia nodded, her resolve hardening. Her powers were growing, her visions clearer, but the weight of her choices loomed larger than ever.

As they stood together in the moonlight, she realized that the fight ahead wasn't just about survival—it was about proving that their love, their bond, was worth defying the heavens themselves.

Chapter

11

THE BURDEN OF CHOICE

The First Choice: The Bridge

Sophia's visions no longer crept up on her—they surged like waves, sometimes catching her mid-conversation, mid-step, or in the middle of class. They blurred the lines between her current life and all the paths she might live.

It began again one rainy afternoon. She had been sitting in the student union café, half-listening to Maddie ramble about an upcoming debate competition, when her vision blurred and the world dropped away.

She saw the bridge again—crumbling, unstable, soaked in rain. Maddie stood in the center, arguing with someone whose face remained hazy. A flash of anger, a slip, and then Maddie's body hit the concrete with a sickening crack.

Sophia's breath caught as reality returned.

"Soph?" Maddie asked, her voice muffled by concern. "Are you okay?"

Sophia stood abruptly. "I need to go."

She arrived at the footbridge ten minutes later, soaked through but too determined to care.

A few minutes later, Maddie appeared, hood up, approaching the same bridge with a guy Sophia vaguely recognized—someone from the political science club.

They were arguing, just like in the vision.

Sophia didn't hesitate. She ran forward. "Maddie, stop!"

Both turned toward her.

"What the hell?" Maddie shouted.

"You can't be here right now," Sophia said, stepping between her friend and the bridge's edge. "It's not safe."

The boy looked confused. "We were just talking—"

"I know," Sophia said quietly. "But if you keep walking, she's going to fall."

Maddie blinked. "Fall? What are you talking about?"

Sophia looked at her, drenched and shaking. "Please, Maddie. Just...trust me."

Maddie looked down at the slick surface beneath her feet, then back at Sophia's face. "Okay," she said finally. "Let's go back."

Later that night, Sophia sat on her bed, wrapped in a blanket, the rain still tapping at the window.

Zephyriel appeared beside her, as if summoned by her thoughts. "You made the right call."

"It changed the outcome," she said, her voice quiet. "But it could've gone the other way."

"Every choice carries risk," he replied. "But this one saved a life."

The Second Choice: The Letter

Another vision came a few days later—this time, about her mother.

She saw Claire sitting at the kitchen table, an unopened envelope resting in front of her. Sophia's name was written on it, and her mother's hands trembled as she hesitated to open it.

Then came two possible futures:

One, her mother read the letter and wept in silence, never speaking to Sophia again.

The other, she never read it—and Sophia remained forever a mystery in her eyes.

It was clear the letter was a confession. A truth Sophia hadn't yet dared to tell: the powers, the visions, Zephyriel.

She sat with the blank page before her for hours, pen in hand.

Zephyriel found her that night. "You saw something again."

She nodded. "My mom. I wrote her a letter. I wanted to tell her everything. But in the vision…no matter what I do, I lose her in some way."

Zephyriel knelt in front of her. "That's the nature of truth. Sometimes it frees us. Sometimes it wounds. But it's always honest."

"I'm not ready to lose her," Sophia said, tears welling in her eyes.

"Then wait," Zephyriel said gently. "There will be a time when she's ready to know. And you'll feel it."

She folded the letter and placed it in her drawer, not sealed, not sent—waiting.

The Third Choice: The Classroom

In a philosophy seminar, her professor launched into a discussion about the illusion of free will.

"As humans," he said, "we believe we have control over our lives. But if all our actions are governed by prior causes—genetics, environment, society—then what choice do we really have?"

Sophia raised her hand, surprising even herself. "We may not control every variable, but we can choose how we respond. That's where our power lies."

The professor tilted his head, intrigued. "You disagree with determinism?"

"I believe in purpose," she said. "I believe we shape our lives through love, sacrifice, and faith. Sometimes we don't see the consequences right away, but our choices ripple far beyond what we can measure."

The room fell silent.

Later, Zephyriel found her outside the building.

"You sounded like someone who's ready to lead," he said.

"I don't feel like a leader," she murmured.

"You are," he said. "And you're becoming more than even I expected."

The Tension Builds

Sophia's powers surged unpredictably now—her visions sharper, her energy stronger, even without focus. Streetlamps flickered when she passed beneath them. Small objects trembled in her dorm room when she felt overwhelmed.

And at night, her dreams darkened. The Council appeared more frequently, their faces blurred but their voices unmistakable. Warnings. Accusations. Ultimatums.

Zephyriel sensed it too.

"The Council won't wait much longer," he said. "They can feel your transformation. And they fear it."

Sophia looked at him, her voice quiet but sure. "Let them."

Chapter

12

HEAVEN MEETS EARTH

Dates, Humanity, and Unexpected Joy

For all the moments Sophia had spent fighting off visions or training her powers, it was the small, human things that reminded her why she was fighting at all. And Zephyriel—who had spent centuries watching from above—was finally stepping into that world with her.

"Let's go on a real date," Sophia said one evening as they lay on the grass outside the dorms, stars twinkling overhead.

Zephyriel raised an eyebrow. "You mean…like mortals do?"

Sophia laughed. "Yes, exactly like mortals do. No energy training. No visions. Just…greasy food and awkward conversation."

"I'm not sure I've ever been awkward," he said with a smirk.

"Oh, I'll make sure of it," she teased, tugging on his shirt playfully.

Date One: Movie-Night Mayhem

Sophia picked the first date: a low-key Friday movie night at a student-run cinema club. She thought it would be simple. Fun. Normal.

She was wrong.

Zephyriel arrived dressed like he'd walked out of a Renaissance painting—buttoned shirt, sleek jacket, and tailored pants. She stared at him for a full minute.

"Do you not own a hoodie?" she asked, laughing.

"I thought this looked… casual."

"Maybe in 1522."

The movie was a cheesy romantic comedy with too many clichés and not enough plot. Zephyriel sat completely still, brow furrowed in concentration, as if he were decoding ancient scripture.

Halfway through, he leaned over and whispered, "Why is everyone pretending they don't know they're in love?"

Sophia stifled a laugh. "That's literally the whole movie."

At the kiss scene, he leaned over again, quieter this time. "Should I be taking notes?"

She turned, wide-eyed. "Are you?"

He smiled. "Mentally."

By the end, her face hurt from laughing—and not at the movie.

Date Two: First Bite of Earthly Sin

Next, she took him to a local diner.

The moment the double bacon cheeseburger hit the table, Zephyriel stared at it like it might be a test from God Himself.

Sophia leaned in. "You're going to love this."

He picked it up carefully, inspecting each layer. "This has...seven components. Possibly eight."

"Eat it, Zeph."

One bite in, and his eyes fluttered closed. "Okay. This might be better than sacred ambrosia."

Sophia burst out laughing. "Don't let the Council hear you say that."

He wiped his mouth with too much dignity for someone eating chili cheese fries and said with complete seriousness, "If this is sin, I understand why humans fall so easily."

Date Three: Laundry-Day Confessions

"I want to show you something really romantic," Sophia said one Saturday.

He raised an eyebrow. "Are we summoning moonlight?"

"No," she grinned. "We're doing laundry."

Twenty minutes later, Zephyriel was staring at a coin-operated washer like it had insulted his ancestors.

"This one requires…exact change?"

Sophia laughed as she fed quarters into the machine. "You've battled shadow wraiths and faced heavenly judgment, but a coin slot baffles you?"

"I do not enjoy being mocked by a machine," he said, crossing his arms.

When the washer started rumbling, he instinctively took a defensive stance.

Sophia grabbed his arm. "It's not possessed. Just old."

When the clothes were tumbling in the dryer and they sat beside each other on the bench, she leaned her head on his shoulder.

"It's weird," she murmured. "This might be my favorite date."

"Even with the demonic appliances?"

"Especially with them."

Falling Harder

They were electric together—when their hands brushed, when their lips met, when their gazes locked across a room.

One evening, after a dinner of street tacos and shared milkshakes, they lay tangled in blankets on Sophia's dorm bed, the faint hum of campus nightlife buzzing outside the window.

Sophia traced her fingers along his collarbone, the space where celestial tattoos shimmered faintly beneath his skin.

"You still glow sometimes," she whispered.

Zephyriel smirked. "Occupational hazard."

Her fingers slid down his chest, slow and deliberate. "Do you… like this life?"

He caught her hand and kissed her knuckles. "I like you in this life."

Their kiss deepened, and the air seemed to shift. Their clothes were shed with unhurried intimacy, laughter mingling with moans, their bodies syncing like their souls already had.

The world fell away.

Nothing existed but warmth, breath, skin, and connection.

Not Heaven. Not Earth. Just them.

Afterglow and Pillow Talk

Later, her head on his chest, she traced lazy circles on his skin.

"You're not who I expected an angel to be," she murmured.

"And you're more than I ever imagined a mortal could be," he said, brushing his lips against her forehead.

"You don't miss the sky?"

He was quiet a moment. "Not when I'm here. Not when I'm with you."

Sophia smiled, content, yet aware that these fleeting moments were built on fragile ground.

Soon, they'd have to fight for every bit of it. But for now, they had tonight—and that was enough.

Chapter

13

LOVE IN THE MIDDLE OF EVERYTHING

Two Worlds, One Coffee Maker

The celestial glow was easy. It was the earthly stuff that got complicated.

Sophia had thought falling in love with a guardian angel would mean constant intensity, soul-gazing, and floating several inches off the ground. And sure, there was some of that. But mostly, it meant explaining things like why laundry pods are not edible or how grocery store self-checkout machines are not trying to test his worthiness.

Especially not at 8:00 a.m. on a Sunday.

"Do you really need three different kinds of oat milk?" Zephyriel asked as they pushed a shopping cart through the store.

Sophia sighed. "Yes, one is for coffee, one is for smoothies, and one is for when I forget I have the other two."

He paused to inspect a bag of sour gummy worms. "These are not natural."

"They're delicious," she corrected.

Later that week, Zephyriel tried to make her breakfast before class. It started with good intentions—and ended with a scorched pan, blackened eggs, and a half-melted spatula.

"I thought divine beings knew how to cook," she teased, wafting smoke away from the fire alarm.

"I protected five different prophets from demonic assassins," he said with perfect seriousness. "None of them required eggs."

Movie Nights and Mortal Mischief

Every Friday night, they made it a ritual to act completely normal: popcorn, bad movies, sweatpants, and snuggles.

One night, Sophia made him watch *The Princess Diaries.*

Zephyriel was transfixed. "Why do they keep trying to hide her power?"

"She's not an angel, she's a teenager."

"Same thing," he murmured.

Sophia laughed so hard she nearly fell off the couch. "That's it. I'm getting you a diary and a tiara."

Another time, they tried karaoke night at a nearby bar. Zephyriel, it turned out, had the voice of an ancient hymn and absolutely zero concept of modern rhythm.

When he chose "Hotline Bling," Sophia nearly spit out her drink.

"Do you even know what this song is about?"

"I believe it's about divine connection through crystal communication lines?"

"Close enough."

He delivered the song like it was a Gregorian chant, causing the bartender to choke on her gum.

Sophia didn't stop laughing for ten minutes.

The Campus Couple

To cover their frequent appearances together, Sophia had told Maddie they were officially dating. Maddie had questions.

"So…is he always this intense?" Maddie asked as they waited in line at the student café, Zephyriel a few paces behind with his arms crossed, guarding like it was a war zone.

"He's very committed to safety," Sophia said diplomatically.

Maddie lowered her voice. "Like…to your safety? Or national security?"

Sophia just smiled and grabbed her latte. "Both. Probably."

Later that week, Maddie caught them kissing in the back corner of the library, surrounded by forgotten philosophy books.

Maddie leaned in, whispered, "Hey, Zeus, if you're gonna ravish my roommate in public, maybe don't do it under the Ethics and Morality section."

Zephyriel turned and blinked. "It felt thematically appropriate."

Glimpses of What's Coming

Despite the humor and joy, Sophia's powers kept reminding her that the world wasn't on pause.

She saw things—brief flashes in her dreams and in waking moments. Visions of her dorm cracked open by celestial fire. A broken blade in Zephyriel's hand. Her own reflection in a mirror, eyes glowing, mouth whispering words she didn't understand.

Sometimes, she saw herself alone. Sometimes, surrounded by flames. And sometimes...victorious.

But always with a cost.

"I'm scared," she admitted one night, curled beside Zephyriel on her twin-sized bed, their limbs entangled awkwardly in the too-small space.

"I am too," he said, pressing his lips to her forehead. "But we'll face it. Together."

The Calm Before the Tempest

In those quiet weeks, Sophia and Zephyriel built something real.

They picnicked in the park. He tried hot sauce and declared it "more unholy than demons."

She made him a playlist and discovered he secretly loved Taylor Swift.

They tried yoga and nearly pulled a muscle laughing in downward dog.

They kissed under stars. They danced in the kitchen. They argued about which Avenger was most morally corrupt.

And every night, as he whispered ancient words into her hair and she curled into his arms, Sophia felt like maybe—maybe—they could have both love and war.

But the visions came again. Clearer. Louder.

The sky would open. The arth would crack. And the Council would descend—merciless and certain.

Sophia woke one night, gasping, clutching her chest.

Zephyriel sat up immediately. "What did you see?"

She looked at him, tears in her eyes. "They're coming. Soon."

His jaw tightened. "Then it's time we stop playing defense."

Sophia nodded, wiping her face. "It's time we prepare for war."

Chapter

14

ALLIES AND WARNINGS

The Strategy for Survival

The laughter, the softness, the human moments—they became the memories Sophia clung to as the storm gathered. Her visions had shifted from fractured glimpses to full, vivid messages. Dreams that were more like prophecies. Warnings. Countdown clocks.

Zephyriel had seen it too. The calm was over.

They no longer trained in the quiet woods but in hidden spaces shielded by Zephyriel's divine sigils—underground tunnels near the library, rooftops after midnight, empty chapels warded with celestial light.

"This isn't just about defense anymore," Zephyriel told her as they stood in an abandoned science building late one night, chalk symbols glowing faintly on the walls. "We have to outthink them. Hit first, not harder—but smarter."

Sophia nodded, winded from channeling a powerful energy burst that cracked a desk in half. "So…you're saying I need to be more chess, less Mortal Kombat."

Zephyriel's lips twitched. "Roughly."

He sketched an arcane diagram in the air—a map of angelic strongholds, weak points in the veil between realms.

"We'll need allies. And sanctuary. Somewhere not even the Council can reach easily."

"Do places like that still exist?" she asked.

He hesitated. "There's one."

A Friend in High Places

They met him in a space that barely clung to reality—a liminal plane between Heaven and Earth. A place where time fluttered and light bent strangely.

His name was Seradiel.

Zephyriel described him as a "former guardian, demoted for compassion." A quiet rebel. A whisper in Heaven's ear.

He appeared in a soft flash of silver and blue, his wings barely visible in the shifting light. He was younger than Zephyriel, or at least he felt younger—wry smile, sharp eyes, the kind of angel who would bring sarcasm to a holy war.

"Zeph," Seradiel said as he emerged from the veil. "Still brooding, I see. And still breaking laws?"

Zephyriel's jaw tightened. "This is Sophia."

Seradiel turned to her, studied her, then nodded slowly. "So...this is the girl Heaven's about to implode over."

Sophia blinked. "I'm flattered?"

"You should be," he said. "The last time someone caused this much celestial drama, we got a whole new Book of Revelations." Despite his humor, his eyes grew serious. "You two have no idea how close they are to open war. You've ignited a philosophical fire. Half the realm thinks Zephyriel's a traitor. The other half wants to crown him a visionary."

"We don't want a war," Sophia said.

Seradiel gave a dry smile. "The thing about revolutions is, you don't always get to choose."

The Warning

Over their next meeting, Seradiel gave them something else: a warning.

"There's a faction forming," he said, leaning over a shimmering celestial map. "Loyal to Eryon, yes—but more militant. They don't just want to punish you. They want to erase what you are. They're not just enforcing the old laws. They want to rewrite them."

Sophia felt a chill run through her. "Why now?"

"Because you changed the equation," he said. "An angel falling in love with a human? That's old scandal. But a human awakening celestial gifts beyond the Archangels themselves? That's an existential crisis."

Zephyriel stood silently, fists clenched.

Seradiel placed a hand on his shoulder. "You can't win this alone."

"So you're with us?" Sophia asked.

Seradiel smirked. "Let's just say I've always liked a good underdog story."

Forming the Resistance

Back on Earth, the real strategy began.

They enlisted the help of others Seradiel quietly directed their way—rogue guardians, celestial scholars, seers in hiding.

Each came with a different gift:

- Tirien, a former Watcher, trained Sophia in the art of divine shielding.
- Mira, a half-human oracle, taught her to control and interpret visions with precision.
- Elias, a mute angel with flaming eyes, could fold space for split-second teleportation.

In the tunnels beneath the old university cathedral, they formed their sanctum.

They called it The Hollow Flame—a space protected by Sophia's light and Seradiel's sigils, invisible to divine sensors.

Sophia's Transformation

Sophia's powers expanded daily. She could now project visions onto surfaces, showing others the futures she saw. Her light had deepened into a radiant gold threaded with silver—a glow Zephyriel called divine resonance.

One night, after a particularly exhausting training session, Sophia collapsed into Zephyriel's arms in their makeshift quarters.

"I feel like I'm becoming someone else," she whispered.

He brushed a thumb along her cheek. "You're becoming more of who you are. Nothing is being taken away."

"Even my humanity?" she asked, her voice cracking.

"That's what anchors you," he said. "That's what saves you."

They kissed, slow and aching. She pulled him closer, grounding herself in the only thing that still felt certain—them.

Tension Before the Break

Seradiel returned a few days later, this time grave.

"They know where you are. A scout from the Council tried to breach the veil but failed. That won't happen twice."

Sophia closed her eyes. "How long do we have?"

"Not long. Days. Maybe hours."

Zephyriel nodded, the room heavy with silence.

"Then let them come," Sophia said, standing tall, light crackling faintly beneath her skin. "Let them see what we've become."

Chapter

15

THE LAST QUIET BEFORE THE STORM

The Hollow Flame was never truly quiet. The underground sanctuary beneath the cathedral had been carved out of ancient stone and divine will—a place between worlds, humming softly with protective sigils. But tonight, there was a stillness that hadn't existed before. The kind that came right before a battle.

Sophia stood in the center chamber, her hands glowing faintly as she traced new runes into the stone floor. Every line she drew pulsed with light, part of the intricate shielding matrix she and Tirien had spent days perfecting.

She was no longer the girl who had wandered into a campus meditation group looking for answers. Her eyes shimmered with knowledge, her aura rippled with power. But her heart still beat with the same human ache—for love, for her friends, for a future that didn't end in fire.

Zephyriel entered the room, armor beginning to form over his celestial form, shadows curling beneath his fingertips. "Everyone's gathering," he said gently. "It's time."

Sophia looked up, nodded, and followed him into the council chamber.

The Inner Circle Gathers

The central sanctuary of The Hollow Flame flickered with blue flame and golden light, powered by Sophia's essence and sealed by Seradiel's glyphs. Around the circular table stood the few who had chosen to defy Heaven for love, loyalty, or the belief that the old laws were broken.

Seradiel stood with arms crossed, wings hidden but presence immense. His tone was uncharacteristically solemn. "They'll come through the western veil—the weakest point. Eryon leads them. He won't negotiate."

Mira, seated with her eyes closed, let out a slow breath. "I've seen them. Clad in light, wielding justice. But there's hesitation in some."

Elias, the mute angel, tapped the stone with the hilt of his blade and then pressed his palm to his chest—a sign that meant willing, no matter the cost.

Tirien leaned on his staff, shaking his head. "Even if they hesitate, they'll strike fast. Their fear of Sophia is greater than their loyalty to reason."

Sophia stepped forward. "Then we show them a reason to stop. We don't just defend—we prove that change is possible."

Zephyriel laid out the tactical plan:

- Mira and Elias would hold the perimeter.
- Tirien would anchor the inner warding.
- Seradiel would guard the only celestial gate in and out.
- Zephyriel and Sophia would meet Eryon directly.

"She needs to see me at my strongest," Sophia said. "Not just powerful—but human. Heart, mind, and soul."

Seradiel looked at her, pride flickering in his gaze. "You're becoming what they feared most—a mortal with divine light, unbroken by rules."

A Moment for Each Other

After the meeting, Sophia and Zephyriel returned to their chamber. The room flickered with candlelight, warm and soft. The sigils on the walls glowed faintly with the pulse of Sophia's presence.

They undressed each other slowly, not out of lust, but out of reverence—memorizing every inch, every scar, every heartbeat. This wasn't the desperate passion of new love. It was something older, deeper, hard-earned.

Afterward, she curled against his chest, listening to the rhythm of a heart that had never belonged on Earth.

"If we don't make it," she whispered.

"We will," he replied.

"But if we don't—"

He turned to her, green eyes blazing. "Then we make this moment eternal."

She kissed him like it was the last time. Maybe it was.

The Final Prep

Sophia walked the sanctuary once more, checking the sigils, reinforcing the protective runes with her own blood and energy. Each glyph responded to her touch now, as if recognizing her as something not just human, not just divine—but something new.

When she reached Mira, the oracle opened her eyes slowly. "You've changed the weave of fate," she said. "Tomorrow was supposed to end in ash. But now…there's a thread of light."

Sophia swallowed. "That's all we need. One thread."

One Last Vision

That night, sleep came reluctantly. When it did, the vision was clear.

She stood on a battlefield of broken stars. Zephyriel fought Eryon, light and shadow clashing in the sky. Sophia stood at the center, hands outstretched, glowing brighter than either of them.

But then came a choice. A door of light opened behind her. Step through it, and she'd ascend—free from pain, immortal, untouchable.

But behind her, the world still burned.

Sophia turned from the light and walked back into the fire.

She woke just before dawn.

Zephyriel sat at the edge of the bed, armored in silver and black, wings fully revealed.

"It's time," he said.

Sophia stood, power humming beneath her skin, and took his hand. "Then let's finish what we started."

Chapter

16

THE FALL OF LIGHT

When the Sky Shattered

It began at dawn.

The air above The Hollow Flame cracked—not with thunder, but with silence. The kind of silence that made the bones ache. Then, a pulse—like a divine heartbeat—rippled outward, bending light, warping time.

Sophia stood at the outer edge of the sanctum, eyes closed, her light connected to every sigil in the network. She could feel the Council's power pressing against her wards. Ancient. Unrelenting. Impossibly cold.

Then came the tear.

A line of pure white light sliced through the western veil. From it, six radiant figures emerged, their wings like fire, their eyes glowing with celestial judgment. At their center stood Eryon, the High Arbiter, halo burning like a sun.

Behind Sophia, Mira whispered, "They're here."

She already knew.

This Is Holy Ground

Zephyriel stepped forward, armor glinting with divine steel, his sword drawn—not in threat, but in promise. "This is sacred ground. You enter uninvited."

Eryon landed with barely a sound, his voice calm, absolute. "There is no sacred ground for traitors. You stand outside the order."

Sophia stepped to Zephyriel's side. Her hair shimmered with silver streaks now, her skin glowing faintly from within. "Then maybe your order needs to fall."

For a heartbeat, Eryon studied her. Then he raised his hand. "Begin."

The First Wave

The Hollow Flame trembled.

From the rift came dozens more—enforcers cloaked in searing white, their weapons shaped from cosmic fire. The sanctum's outer wards flared to life, golden light pushing against the onslaught.

Mira raised her staff and called out, her voice echoing through the chamber. "Elias—now!"

With a burst of red light, Elias appeared in the air, teleporting between attackers, disarming them in flashes of fire and speed. His movements were a dance of controlled rage.

Sophia focused her energy, sending bursts of shielding light outward to reinforce the barrier, buying them time.

Zephyriel moved like a storm—striking, defending, protecting. His blade sang with each clash, his face unreadable but his heart burning in every swing.

Holding the Line

Tirien chanted beneath his breath, roots of divine energy crawling up the chamber walls. "The veil won't hold much longer," he grunted. "They're ripping through space itself."

Sophia's vision blurred. She saw a fracture forming in the southern wall—too many enforcers, too fast.

She raised both hands, summoning a blinding orb of energy and slamming it into the breach. It exploded in a shockwave of light and sound, buying seconds—precious seconds.

"Fall back to the second chamber!" Zephyriel called.

Seradiel appeared beside him, bleeding from a wound in his shoulder, but grinning. "Told you this place wouldn't stay hidden forever."

Zephyriel growled, "Not the time for 'I told you so,' Seradiel."

The Turning Point

Sophia and Zephyriel reached the center of The Hollow Flame, where the true heart of the sanctum pulsed.

"We make our stand here," Zephyriel said.

Sophia nodded. Her power surged, cracking the stone beneath her feet. She was beyond mortal now—something new. A hybrid of love, light, and defiance.

Eryon descended before them. He walked, not flew, his presence bending the space around him.

"You were given protection, Sophia Ardent," he said, voice sharp. "And you abused it."

"I never asked for protection," she answered. "Only truth. And love."

"You have perverted both," he hissed, drawing his blade—a weapon forged from the edge of the first star.

Zephyriel stepped in front of her, blade raised. "You'll have to go through me."

Eryon didn't answer. He attacked.

Clash of Powers

The chamber exploded in light as Zephyriel and Eryon collided— blade against blade, Heaven's fury against the fury of the heart. Sparks flew, dust and ash rising from the ground.

Sophia watched for only a moment before she turned—defending Mira from an enforcer who had broken through. She reached inside herself, grasping the core of her power, and released it in a wave that knocked the enforcer backward with force that cracked the stone walls.

Tirien went down, shielding three others with his body. Seradiel dove to protect him, throwing up a barrier just in time to absorb a searing celestial spear.

Sophia's vision blurred again—this time unbidden.

She saw Zephyriel, on his knees, blood on his lips.

She saw Eryon raising his sword.

She saw herself scream, light erupting from her body like a star.

She saw the Council…hesitate.

Now or Never

The vision snapped away.

Sophia ran to the center of the chamber. "Everyone—fall back!" she shouted.

Eryon struck Zephyriel to the ground.

"You don't belong here," he said, raising his sword.

Sophia's voice rang out. "No. You don't."

She stepped between them, light blazing from her palms.

"I won't let you take him."

The light grew—filling the chamber, lifting her off the ground.

"You fear me," she said. "Not because I broke the law. But because I proved it can be broken."Her voice boomed, laced with divine force. "You want to judge me? Then see me."

And for one perfect moment, she showed them everything—her visions, her pain, her love. The Council saw her humanity and her power not as opposites, but as one.

End of the Battle... for Now

The Council faltered. Eryon lowered his blade.

Sophia collapsed, caught by Zephyriel before she hit the floor.

"She lives," Seradiel whispered, exhausted. "And she just made history."

The Council retreated into the veil. No final threat. No last decree. Only silence.

Aftermath

Sophia lay still, recovering, her light dim but steady.

Zephyriel sat beside her, holding her hand, eyes shining with awe and fear. "You became something they couldn't fight," he whispered.

Sophia's voice was weak but clear. "I didn't beat them. I made them see."

Chapter

17

FRACTURES IN HEAVEN

The Council Reassembles

The chamber known as The Skyhold floated high above the celestial plane, constructed from translucent white stone and humming with ancient energy. It was where laws were written, decrees passed, and judgment rendered.

After centuries of unity, the Council stood fractured.

The great hall was darker than usual, the halos of the attending angels dimmed in silent protest or troubled contemplation. Their golden mantles hung heavier today.

Eryon stood at the center dais, face impassive, hands behind his back. But even he could not hide the tension radiating from him.

"She broke no law," said Saeliel, one of the High Council's oldest and most revered voices. "And yet you sought to destroy her."

"She didn't need to break the law," Eryon replied coolly. "Her existence challenges it. Her very being threatens everything we've upheld for millennia."

"She is mortal," argued Thamael, wings folded tightly behind him. "And yet she deflected our might. She shone with the light of the Veil itself. She is something new. Perhaps she is what was promised in the old scrolls—the Light of Choice."

Murmurs broke out across the chamber.

Eryon's eyes narrowed. "And what of Zephyriel? He knew what he was doing. He corrupted his ward. He defiled the ancient bond."

"Or elevated it," Saeliel said calmly. "There is a difference between defiance and evolution."

"He is not a revolutionary," Eryon snapped. "He is a traitor who seduced a human and endangered the balance between Heaven and Earth. If we do nothing, others will follow. The Veil will tear.

Cracks in the Council

The Council divided silently into factions:

- Those who still clung to the Old Order, led by Eryon.
- Those who saw Sophia as the beginning of something new—a bridge, not a threat.
- And a growing number who stood uncertain, shaken by the light they had seen within her.

"She showed us everything," Thamael said, stepping forward. "Her thoughts, her pain, her hope. She didn't fight with rage—she fought with truth. Can you not see it?"

"She is dangerous," Eryon thundered. "She tore through our enforcers. She could have destroyed us—and chose not to."

"That is exactly why she deserves to be heard," Saeliel said. "Her restraint was not weakness—it was wisdom."

But Eryon wasn't listening. His pride had been wounded, his authority questioned for the first time in an age. And he would not let it go unanswered.

Chapter

18

THE HEART, THE LIGHT, THE COST

In the Glow of Victory

Days after the battle at The Hollow Flame, the world above moved on as if nothing had changed. Students returned to campus. Professors handed out midterm prep guides. Maddie ranted about cafeteria food like the heavens hadn't cracked open above them just nights before.

But beneath the surface, in the sanctum of carved sigils and quiet whispers, everything was different.

Sophia stood in the morning light, overlooking the crumbled western corner of The Hollow Flame. Repairs had begun, slowly, but there was something reverent about the way the damage was being left visible—like a scar worn with pride.

Zephyriel approached behind her, his touch gentle on her back. "The veil is holding."

Sophia nodded. "For now."

They shared a look. No more illusions. The Council hadn't spoken again, hadn't retaliated. But their silence was not surrender. It was strategy.

Still, there was peace—for now.

A Night Like Any Other—and Not

To celebrate the safety they had won, Mira and Tirien insisted on hosting a "half-mortal victory dinner." The angles used a glamour to make themselves look mortal. Maddie was even invited—though she believed the story that this was an off-campus "graduate spiritual society."

Elias prepared the food (it turned out angels make incredible roasted potatoes), and Seradiel passed around celestial wine in cracked goblets. Laughter echoed off stone and starlight, something rare and deeply human in this half-holy place.

Sophia leaned into Zephyriel, both of them sitting on a makeshift cushion against the wall.

"You ever think," she murmured, "that this is what Heaven was supposed to be?"

Zephyriel looked around—the laughter, the shared stories, the unity between people who should never have met, let alone fought together.

"Maybe," he said. "Or maybe we're building something better."

The First Fracture

That night, Sophia dreamed again.

But it wasn't a vision—it was a warning.

She stood in a mirror room, dozens of versions of herself staring back. In each reflection, something was missing. A hand. A voice. A heart. In the one that held her gaze the longest, she stood alone.

No Zephyriel.

She woke with a start, breath sharp, the sheets tangled. Beside her, he stirred instantly.

"Another dream?"

She nodded, sitting up. "It was different. It wasn't about the Council."

He studied her, quiet. Then he said what she hadn't wanted to hear: "It was about me, wasn't it?"

Her silence was answer enough.

The Trap Set in Light

The next day, Zephyriel vanished.

He was supposed to meet her at the southern watchpoint. When he didn't appear, Sophia's stomach dropped. She felt no danger, no rupture in the veil—but that absence was worse.

She reached for the bond they shared—the pull that tied their souls together—and felt only resistance. As if something was…muting it.

"Mira," she said, rushing into the sanctum. "Something's wrong."

The oracle was already standing, her eyes white with Sight. "They've taken him," she whispered. "They used light as a cage. They inverted your bond—used your connection to locate and bind him."

Sophia's knees nearly buckled.

"No," she breathed. "They wouldn't—"

"They did," Seradiel said, appearing behind her, jaw clenched. "They couldn't defeat you, so they took him instead."

A Final Decision

Sophia stood at the edge of the cracked altar, her power sparking through her veins. Her fear warred with fury, and her visions shifted violently behind her eyes—burning futures, splintering timelines.

"You can't go after him alone," Seradiel warned.

"I'm not going after him," she said. "I'm going to bring him home."

Maddie appeared at the doorway, worry etched across her face. "Sophia…what is happening?"

Sophia turned, her glow too bright now to hide, her voice steady but raw. "Everything's changed. I have to go."

"To him?"

"To who I am now," Sophia said. "And yes. To him."

The Cliff's Edge

Sophia's vision: She stood alone beneath a dark sky. A gate formed in front of her—carved from light and memory, forged by love and betrayal.

Behind it lay the heavens. And Zephyriel.

As she reached for the handle, her voice was calm. "They stole him to break me. They forgot…I don't break. I burn."

With one final breath, she stepped through.

Chapter

19

SECRETS SHARED

The late afternoon sun poured through the dorm window, bathing Sophia's room in warm gold. The scent of coffee lingered faintly in the air—Maddie's doing, as usual—and the hum of campus life drifted up from the quad below. For the first time in weeks, Sophia could relax, though a small, tight knot of anxiety remained in her chest. Zephyriel was gone, and the emptiness of his absence was as heavy as any iron chain.

Maddie sprawled across the bed, scrolling through her phone, her legs swinging idly. "So, finals are next week," she said casually. "You're studying, right? Or are you still…you know…glowing and stuff?"

Sophia rolled her eyes but smiled. "I'm studying. Mostly. But I have other…things to think about."

Maddie tilted her head. "Other things? Sophia, I swear, you've been acting weird since…you know, everything."

Sophia hesitated, the words pressing against her chest like they might burst out if she didn't speak soon. She glanced at Maddie, that one constant in her life, the sister she'd chosen. The one person who deserved to know the truth.

"I need to tell you something," she said finally. "Something big. And it's…it might sound insane."

Maddie sat up, her curiosity immediately piqued. "Okay. I'm ready. Hit me with it."

Sophia took a deep breath. "I…I have powers. Real ones. Spiritual ones. I can see things others can't. And…I'm not alone in this. Zephyriel…he's not just a guy I'm dating. He's my guardian angel."

Maddie blinked. Then blinked again. And finally let out a loud, disbelieving laugh. "You're joking, right? Like…this isn't some cosplay thing or a prank?"

Sophia shook her head. "I swear it. And I can show you."

With a wave of her hand, the air in the room shimmered slightly, like sunlight through water. Maddie's jaw fell open as she saw the faint outline of light tracing over Sophia's skin, the glow pulsing from her chest.

"Okay," she whispered. "Okay, wow. You're…you're like a superhero or something."

"It's more than that," Sophia said softly. "And I need your help. Zephyriel…he's been taken. The Council—they're after us. They want him locked away."

Maddie stared at her, wide-eyed. "Wait, wait, wait…*the Council?* Like angels?"

Sophia nodded. "Yes. And we're going to have to plan a rescue. I can't do it alone."

For the first time, Maddie's expression softened. She sat beside Sophia and grabbed her hand. "Then we do it together. Whatever it takes."

Life Amidst Chaos

The following weeks were a strange balance of ordinary life and the extraordinary. Finals loomed, and Sophia spent long hours in the library with Maddie at her side, studying calculus and philosophy while occasionally disappearing to trace sigils of protection across their dorm room walls.

Her parents visited for the weekend, unaware of the hidden light in their daughter's eyes. Sophia smiled, laughed, and shared stories of her classes, careful to omit any mention of angels or battles in the heavens. The contrast between the ordinary—family dinners, campus gossip, dorm life—and the divine struggle she now lived with was dizzying.

But slowly, Maddie adapted. She learned to read the subtle signs when Sophia's powers flared, when her visions tugged at her thoughts, and even began helping her decipher small glimpses of potential futures. Their bond deepened, not just as friends, but as coconspirators in a plan that was growing ever more dangerous.

Glimpses of the Future

One night, Sophia collapsed onto her bed after a long study session, visions flickering behind her eyelids. She saw Zephyriel chained in golden light, the walls of his prison twisting like mirrored flames. She saw herself walking through the celestial gate—a gate no human had ever survived—and felt the pull of countless outcomes stretching before her.

Some showed her failing, her powers not enough to save him. Others glimmered with hope: She reached him, freed him, and together they struck a blow against the Council's rigid power.

She shivered. The visions were growing more vivid, more detailed, affecting her decisions even in mundane moments: which classes to take, which friends to trust, what meals to eat to keep her energy steady. Every choice mattered now, and even a casual decision could ripple through outcomes in ways she couldn't yet fully predict.

A Summer of Planning

When finals ended and the campus emptied for summer break, Sophia finally allowed herself the time to plan. With Maddie by her side, they explored texts Zephyriel had left behind, small clues about celestial law, ancient maps of Heaven, and possible hidden gateways.

"None of this is simple," Maddie said as they pored over a glowing celestial chart one evening. "I mean, humans can't even *enter* the divine realm without...like, dying or going insane."

Sophia nodded. "I know. That's why it has to be careful. Step by step. I can't just rush in and grab him. I have to learn, train, and...we have to be clever. We need allies."

"Allies in Heaven?" Maddie asked, raising an eyebrow.

Sophia smiled faintly. "One step at a time. There's someone there who might help. Someone who's been questioning the old rules for a while. Zephyriel hinted at it...I just have to reach them."

And with that, the summer stretched before them—a fragile time of preparation, secrecy, and deepening friendship. As Sophia's powers continued to grow, Maddie began learning the first rules of the celestial struggle, and the looming challenge of rescuing Zephyriel became a plan in motion.

Chapter

20

THE HOLLOW FLAME

The air beneath the cathedral was cool and damp, carrying the scent of aged stone and candle wax. Sophia's footsteps echoed softly along the winding staircase carved into the catacombs, Maddie just behind her, eyes wide as they descended.

"This is...insane," Maddie whispered. "I mean, really insane. Are you sure it's safe?"

Sophia smiled, a mix of nerves and excitement curling in her chest. "As safe as it can be. This place—the Hollow Flame—it's where angels who oppose the Council meet. It's where we'll plan to rescue Zephyriel. And now, it's where you come in."

Maddie swallowed hard, her hand brushing against the stone wall. "You really think I can do this? I'm...me. A college student, not some celestial spy."

"You've got more courage than you know," Sophia said firmly. "And you're my anchor. Zephyriel can't be saved without someone like you watching my back."

The spiral staircase under the cathedral twisted downward into shadow, but Sophia walked confidently, Maddie trailing behind, muttering under her breath.

"I still don't understand why the 'Hollow Flame' sounds like some edgy fantasy nightclub instead of, you know, a supersecret rebel base," Maddie whispered, rolling her eyes.

Sophia grinned. "Because it *is* edgy. And fantasy. But you'll get used to it."

Maddie shook her head, brushing her hair out of her face. "I am *never* getting used to this. I have finals next week, and somehow I'm also moonlighting as an angelic freedom fighter. I didn't even pass my last calculus test. What if I mess this up?"

"You're not going to mess this up," Sophia said, squeezing her shoulder. "And if you do... well, we've got Seradiel to bail us out."

They rounded the final corner and stepped into the Hollow Flame. The cavern was vast, glowing with floating orbs of golden light that bobbed in the air, illuminating ancient celestial maps etched into the stone walls. A faint hum of energy reverberated beneath their feet, vibrating through the stone as if the place itself were alive.

At the long, curved table in the center of the chamber stood Seradiel. Maddie froze mid-step. The angel was massive, his muscles corded like carved marble, tattoos of gold spiraling across his dark skin in intricate patterns that shimmered faintly in the glowing light. His gray dreadlocks hung past his shoulders, framing a face so handsome it was almost impossible to look at without getting distracted. And his eyes—gray-blue, sharp, and piercing—tracked her every movement.

Maddie raised an eyebrow. "Oh yeah, Seradiel. Speaking of...can we talk about how your angel friend is basically ripped enough to be a Marvel character with tattoos that glow and gray dreadlocks that somehow make him look cooler than everyone else combined?"

Sophia couldn't help laughing. "He's a serious force, Maddie. And yes, he looks intimidating. But he's...more than that. You'll see."

Maddie swallowed. "Okay...that's...wow. Yeah, definitely a Marvel character."

Seradiel's lips curved in a faint smile as he strode forward, each step exuding calm power.

"You must be Maddie," he said, voice deep and smooth, rumbling like distant thunder. "Sophia has told me much about you. I hope your humor is as strong as your loyalty."

Maddie extended a hand with a grin. "Well, I can make sarcastic jokes in any tense life-or-death scenario. Does that count?"

Seradiel chuckled—a rich, deep sound that made Maddie's stomach flip. "It counts. Welcome to the Hollow Flame."

Sophia's nerves fluttered. Maddie's energy, her laughter, and even her irreverence somehow grounded Seradiel in a way that Sophia hadn't expected. She watched her friend bravely banter with an angelic being, the way Maddie always seemed to break tension with humor.

At the head of the table stood a figure with silver hair and eyes that seemed to hold storms—Seradiel. The aura around him was calm, grounded, but commanding. Maddie couldn't look away.

Sophia took a deep breath. "Everyone, this is Maddie. My best friend—and now, part of the plan."

The angels' gazes swept over Maddie, some curious, some skeptical.

Seradiel stepped forward, offering a hand. "Welcome, Maddie. Sophia speaks highly of you. I hope we'll see that you're as brave as she says."

Maddie's heart thumped as she shook his hand. "I…I'll do my best."

And for the first time, she felt it—the pulse of something greater, a purpose that was hers as much as Sophia's.

The Resistance

Seradiel led them deeper into the sanctuary, showing Maddie the operational heart of the Resistance. Celestial maps glowed on the walls, constellations of angelic factions flickering with every movement. Holographic projections showed portals between realms, angelic patrols, and council strongholds.

"This is where we plan our moves," Seradiel explained, his voice steady. "The Council believes they control everything. They are wrong."

Maddie squinted at a glowing map. "So…wait. You're saying we're basically planning a heist…*on Heaven*?"

Seradiel's sharp gray-blue eyes flicked to her, a smile tugging at the corner of his lips. "Yes. But it is no laughing matter. This is dangerous."

"Yeah, but it *is* hilarious to me," Maddie muttered, grinning. "I mean, I get to plan a top-secret break-in with angels? This is better than any final exam I'll ever take…probably."

Sophia laughed, relieved at Maddie's humor cutting through the tension.

Seradiel's expression softened slightly, but his gaze remained thoughtful.

"Humor is a weapon," he said, almost to himself. "It reminds us why we fight. Never underestimate it."

Connections in the Shadows

Over the next week, Maddie became more comfortable in the Hollow Flame. She trained with Seradiel daily, learning to sense celestial energies, wield basic defensive maneuvers, and understand the flows of magic that permeated the Hollow Flame.

Their interactions were playful yet focused:

- Maddie kept tripping over the faintly glowing symbols on the floor. "Why are the floors always trying to kill me?"
- Seradiel would catch her, muscles like stone under her hands, and gently tease: "You step where you are told."
- Maddie would snort. "Right, because the glowing lines scream, 'Don't step here, Human!' Not obvious at all."

Despite the teasing, their bond deepened. Seradiel taught her the subtle art of reading celestial energy, explaining, "Even angels must respect the flow of power. You are human, but with Sophia's guidance, you can manipulate energy without losing yourself."

Maddie's laughter often punctuated the lessons. "Okay, so I'm like a magical cat trying not to knock over the cosmic vase?"

"Yes," Seradiel said, smirking. "Exactly like that."

Planning the Rescue

With Sophia's visions and Maddie's humor keeping the team grounded, the Hollow Flame became a hive of preparation:

- *Mapping celestial planes*: Sophia and Maddie traced safe pathways to enter the heavenly plane, accounting for Council patrols and unstable portals.
- *Recruiting allies*: They identified angels sympathetic to their cause, discreetly reaching out through coded messages and trusted contacts.
- *Strategic simulations*: Using holographic models, they tested potential outcomes of infiltrating the Council's strongholds.

And throughout it all, Maddie and Seradiel's bond grew. Late nights spent poring over maps often ended with quiet smiles, light teasing, and touches that lingered just a second too long.

Maddie muttered one evening, exhausted but grinning: "I swear, if Sophia hadn't dragged me into this…I would never have had a crush on a six-foot-tall, tattooed, gray-dreadlocked angel. But here we are."

Seradiel's gaze softened, the corners of his mouth lifting. "You are remarkable, Maddie. Courageous, clever…and unafraid to laugh even in darkness. That will serve you well."

They turned a corner, and the hidden entrance to a cavernous space opened before them. The Hollow Flame was larger than Maddie expected, lit with soft, golden light emanating from floating orbs that hovered above stone pedestals. The ceiling arched high above, dripping with stalactites that glimmered like faint constellations. Around a long, curved table stood several figures—tall, radiant, and distinctly angelic, yet with a wariness in their eyes that mirrored Sophia's own.

Connections in the Shadows

Days passed, and Maddie settled into the rhythm of the Hollow Flame. She trained with Seradiel, learning to sense the celestial energy that surrounded them, practicing defensive techniques, and studying the histories of angels who had dared to oppose the Council.

Their bond deepened quickly, subtle sparks of flirtation and gentle teasing blending with the intensity of their work.

One evening, as they pored over maps detailing potential gateways, Maddie caught Seradiel's hand brushing hers.

"You're a natural at this," he murmured, eyes glinting green in the dim light.

"Am I?" Maddie said, heart racing, trying to mask the flush creeping up her neck. "I don't even know if I can do this."

Seradiel's grin was patient but sharp. "You can. You've got courage, and you've got Sophia on your side. That's enough for now. For the rest…we'll see."

Chapter

21

STRENGTH IN SHADOWS

The Hollow Flame buzzed with energy as Sophia paced the central chamber, Maddie leaning casually against the edge of a glowing map table, smirking.

"You really need to stop doing that thing with your hands when you think," Maddie said. "It makes you look like a frustrated conductor of celestial chaos."

Sophia exhaled, letting her fingers drift through the air. Golden threads of energy rose at her command, hovering and curling like liquid sunlight. "Frustrated conductor of celestial chaos? I *like* that. But I'm not frustrated. Just…focused."

Maddie snorted. "Uh-huh. Focused. That's what they'll say when we all get blown to kingdom come. Totally focused."

Sophia rolled her eyes, but even she couldn't suppress a grin. Humor always had a way of keeping her grounded, even when her visions— fragments of possible futures—made her chest tighten.

Training Intensifies

Zephyriel's presence in the Hollow Flame was subtle but constant. He hovered at the edge of her awareness, invisible to Maddie but felt in every flicker of energy around her.

"Focus on your energy flow," he instructed, his deep voice resonating inside her mind.

Sophia followed his guidance, moving her hands slowly, letting strands of golden light intertwine with the shadowed currents of the Hollow Flame.

"You're ready for glimpses," Zephyriel continued, stepping closer, green eyes locking with hers. "The Council will act, and you must anticipate their moves. You will see potential futures—not all of them certain, but enough to guide your choices."

Her first attempt at a vision came in a flash of heat and sound. She saw Maddie laughing at Seradiel's jokes in the Hollow Flame, a familiar scene—but it suddenly shifted. Shadowed figures of angels surrounded them, weapons drawn. Maddie froze, unsure, her humor failing her in the darkness. Sophia gasped and snapped back to the present.

"Too soon," Zephyriel said softly, placing a hand on her shoulder. "You must focus without fear. You can see what *may* come, not what will come. This is why I have stayed close all these years."

Sophia's chest tightened. "All these years…you've been watching me?"

"Yes," he said simply. "Since the moment you were born, you were mine to protect. But now, you are becoming more than a child under my watch. You are a force. And soon, the Council will realize this too."

Maddie and Seradiel: Humor in the Storm

Meanwhile, Maddie and Seradiel had carved out their own corner of the Hollow Flame, plotting diversion strategies for the resistance and occasionally getting distracted by playful banter.

Maddie smirked at a celestial map, pointing to a swirling portal. "So you're saying we just… jump through here and hope no one notices?"

Seradiel's gray-blue eyes narrowed. "Not 'hope,' human. Strategy, timing, precision. You must treat each step with respect for what lies beyond."

Maddie leaned closer, tilting her head. "Respect, got it. But what if…I trip? Or sneeze?"

"You will not sneeze," Seradiel said, his lips twitching despite his stern tone. "And if you trip, I will catch you."

Maddie's grin widened. "You *will*, huh? Not like you have a choice, tall, tattooed celestial man."

Seradiel chuckled, the sound low and musical. "Perhaps."

Hours passed in laughter, planning, and training. Even in these moments, Sophia could sense the bond between her two closest allies strengthening—a tether of humor and trust, which would be crucial in the coming chaos.

Seeds of Danger

Later, Sophia sat cross-legged on a raised platform, Maddie beside her, Zephyriel's energy flowing invisibly around her. She reached out, focusing on her visions again. Golden light coiled around her fingertips as glimpses of futures flashed—Council patrols intercepting angels, corridors of heavenly power shifting, possible confrontations where allies faltered or betrayed them.

"I can see them," Sophia whispered. "I can feel what *may* happen… the Council is preparing. Their next move will be swift."

Zephyriel's voice, soft but urgent, echoed in her mind. "We must anticipate, adapt, and resist. Every decision you make now…affects the outcome. Trust your visions, Sophia. Trust yourself."

Maddie leaned in, nudging her shoulder. "Also, don't forget to eat. You're glowing, but you still need real food. Celestial power doesn't cancel out snacks."

Sophia laughed, letting tension slip for a moment. "Noted."

Zephyriel's green eyes softened as he watched them from the shadows. "You teach them humanity as much as I teach them power," he said quietly to himself. "That is your greatest strength."

The Hollow Flame pulsed with quiet energy, every corner alive with golden and silver light, flickering along with soft murmurs of angels in discussion. Sophia walked along the stone platforms suspended above the glowing maps, her hands tracing the lines of energy that wove together the sanctuary like a living web. She had been practicing daily, guided by Zephyriel's steady, green-eyed presence—both terrifying and comforting all at once.

Maddie lounged on one of the benches, arms crossed and smirking. "So you're telling me all this…magic, glowing maps, and hand-waving is going to get us into Heaven? And you've never once blown yourself up?"

Sophia scowled playfully. "It's called control. Precision. And...I haven't yet."

Maddie raised an eyebrow. "Yet is the scary part."

Seradiel, standing nearby, arms crossed over his broad chest, golden tattoos catching the light, gray dreadlocks swaying as he moved, gave a rumbling chuckle. "The human's humor is relentless."

"She keeps me sane," Sophia said softly, glancing at Maddie.

Maddie winked. "And I keep her alive. I'm basically a superhero. Sidekick, obviously."

Seradiel shook his head, but the corners of his lips twitched. "You are... fortunate to have each other."

Meeting the Resistance

Sophia turned to the group of angels gathered around a large circular table, the surface glowing with shifting celestial maps. Zephyriel had brought her here not just to train, but to meet the other members of the resistance—a select few who had quietly opposed the Council's rigid enforcement of the old laws.

"This is Lysariel," Seradiel said, gesturing to a lithe angel with silver hair and sharp blue eyes, wings tipped with violet. "She specializes in reconnaissance—moving unseen through the human and celestial planes. She'll teach you how to read energies without being detected."

Lysariel inclined her head, smiling faintly. "Your energy is strong already. You may surprise even yourself."

Next, Seradiel introduced Thalor, a stocky angel with bronze skin and wide, amber eyes. His strength was legendary among the resistance.

"I teach defensive and combat applications," Thalor said simply, offering a hand that Sophia instinctively felt the need to grasp—but didn't, just in case he was testing her.

Finally, there was Arelis, a soft-spoken, smaller angel with dark hair and eyes like molten gold. "I manage the information network. Messages, codes, movements—anything we cannot reveal openly to humans. You will work with me to decipher...signals."

Sophia's mind raced. Every angel had a specialty, a skill critical to their resistance. And somehow, she had to coordinate with them—all while developing powers that could rival theirs.

Maddie leaned against a pillar, whispering to Sophia, "Okay, so if I get killed, I assume there's a backup plan? Like…a magical hazard insurance policy?"

Sophia laughed softly, squeezing her hand. "Don't joke about that. But yes, we have contingencies."

Seradiel shook his head again, though his grin betrayed him. "The human is unbearable."

"Oh, thank you," Maddie said cheerfully. "I pride myself on it."

Training in Teams

Seradiel guided Sophia through the first group training exercise. Each angel demonstrated a skill, and Sophia attempted to replicate or counter it using her own growing abilities. Lysariel darted across the room with such speed that her silver hair became a streak; Thalor launched phantom strikes of energy, testing Sophia's reflexes; Arelis created holographic traps in the air that twisted around her like vines.

Maddie stood on the sidelines, commentary running nonstop. "Look at her go! Who knew hand-waving could be a weapon? Also, Lysariel, slow down! You're giving the poor girl whiplash!"

Seradiel growled in mock irritation. "Control yourself, human. This is serious."

"Seradiel, you're hilarious when you're angry. You should do comedy. Or not. Probably safer for the world if you don't." Maddie grinned.

Sophia found herself laughing despite the intensity of training. Humor wasn't just comic relief—it was a tether to the world she was trying to save.

Banter, Tension, and a Spark

After the first round, Sophia and Seradiel were paired off for a defensive drill. Maddie hovered behind Seradiel, hands on hips. "Ohhh, Seradiel versus the human girl. Bet she gets wrecked. Or you, actually."

Seradiel's gray-blue eyes glinted. "Do not underestimate her."

"Yeah, well... I am a master at comic distraction," Maddie said, spinning around to swing a stick at a practice dummy. "This counts as serious, right?"

Sophia smirked at Seradiel who had been watching silently from across the room. The gray of his eyes deepened with amusement. "She will test you," he said softly. "In every way."

"Every way," Maddie echoed innocently. "Especially emotionally. I'm like...emotional napalm. Totally unintentional."

Plotting the Next Move

After the exercises, Sophia gathered with Seradiel, Maddie, and the resistance members. Celestial maps hovered before them, showing potential access points into the heavenly plane and zones patrolled by the Council.

"This is where you come in, human," Lysariel said, glancing at Maddie. "You will assist in identifying weak points. Your presence will anchor Sophia while she maintains the portal. But you must not... become...overwhelmed. The heavenly plane can be...dangerous to mortals."

"Oh, no pressure," Maddie quipped, waving her hands. "Piece of cake. Easy stuff. Just...walking into the ultimate realm of divine beings and not dying. Got it."

Sophia grinned. "You always make me laugh when I want to cry."

Seradiel rolled his eyes, muttering under his breath. "She is unbearable."

"Unbearable...but adorable!" Maddie added cheerfully, spinning away.

As the trio continued strategizing late into the night, Sophia's visions flickered violently, images overlapping—Zephyriel, trapped, wounded; Maddie, in danger; angels in rebellion; the Council descending.

And through it all, a voice in the shadows whispered in a language only Sophia could hear.

"The veil is breaking...and your choices will decide the fate of all."

Sophia's breath caught. Even Maddie, with her humor and light, sensed the weight in the air.

The storm was coming. And nothing in the Hollow Flame would be safe for long.

Sophia stared at the glowing celestial lines, threading together potential strategies, and preparing Maddie for the reality of her role. Every laugh, every jibe, every spark of humor and camaraderie was a lifeline. The Hollow Flame wasn't just a sanctuary—it was a family, a resistance, and a preparation ground for the inevitable storm to come.

She felt Zephyriel's presence, just a whisper of energy, and she knew: The Council would strike, the heavenly realm would resist, and she would have to make impossible choices.

But here, surrounded by laughter, friendship, and the first faint hints of rebellion, Sophia felt...ready.

22

THE THREADS BETWEEN

The Hollow Flame was alive with quiet energy, the soft hum of celestial power vibrating through the walls of the underground sanctuary beneath the cathedral. Sophia stood in the center of the main chamber, arms outstretched, trying to stabilize the threads of light that wove around her.

Zephyriel wasn't beside her this time. Not physically. Not in the way she wanted. Her heart ached for him—imprisoned in the Heavenly Realm, facing the Council's punishments—and the telepathic connection that once allowed their constant whispers and touches was now fleeting. Most of the time, she only caught flashes of his presence: A word, a green gaze, a pulse of warmth that reminded her he was still fighting, still there.

"Sophia…you can do this," he whispered suddenly in her mind. The connection lasted only a second, and then he was gone, leaving her gasping, clutching the air as if she could pull him closer.

"I swear," Sophia muttered aloud, spinning around, half expecting to see him materialize. "If I get up there and find you, Zeph, I'm going to—ugh—I'm going to hug you until you explode."

Maddie, perched on the edge of a floating platform with a cup of what she insisted was "emergency coffee" teetering in her hand, grinned. "Well, I hope he likes hugs because you look like a desperate human attacking a large, glowing angel statue."

"Emergency coffee?" Sophia asked, raising an eyebrow.

"Very much so. Apparently, mortal caffeine is required when angels start waving their hands and making the whole room vibrate. Trust me, it's a thing," Maddie said, plopping herself down on the edge of the platform.

Seradiel leaned against the rail, "It's a weak thing. Mortal caffeine."

"Oh, don't start," Maddie shot back. "You clearly don't understand the mortal mind. Or our digestive system."

Sophia shot her a glare. "Desperate is…okay. And he's not a statue!"

Seradiel, arms crossed, muscles flexing beneath the golden tattoos that ran across his bronzed skin, let out a low chuckle. "He is in the Heavenly Realm, Sophia. You can yell at him all you want, but—"

"Yeah, yeah, I get it," Sophia cut in, exasperated. "I can't hug him right now. But that doesn't mean I won't plan to rescue him."

Maddie smirked, taking a sip of her coffee. "Oh, rescue missions, I like this! Adventure, danger, and you get to boss everyone around. I see your life choices clearly now."

Seradiel rolled his gray-blue eyes. "You do realize this is dangerous. Literally impossible. And you—"

"Relax," Maddie said, wagging a finger. "I'm here to keep spirits high. That's my official role. I do comedy, sarcasm, and occasionally chaos."

Sophia let out a small laugh despite the tension in her chest. It helped, to have Maddie and Seradiel there, grounding her, giving her a reminder of life beyond worry and imprisonment

Planning the Rescue

The council's interference had forced the resistance to become sharper, more coordinated. Sophia gathered with Zephyriel's allies, huddled around celestial maps projected in soft light, their threads of magic shimmering in the chamber.

"Here," Lysariel said, pointing to a glowing node in the map. "Council patrols are heaviest here. If we attempt entry through this route, your connection to Zephyriel will be disrupted almost entirely."

Sophia frowned. "Then…we have to find a way to maintain contact. If he weakens too much, I might lose him completely."

Seradiel stepped forward. "I've devised a method to channel his energy through a proxy angel—someone who can stabilize the link. But it's risky. If the Council detects it…" His voice dropped, and Maddie's grin faded just a little.

"Risky, dangerous, or completely crazy?" Maddie asked, clearly teasing but gripping the edge of the platform.

"Choose one," Seradiel said flatly, though a faint smile tugged at his lips.

Maddie winked at Sophia. "Well then, let's do all three. I like to keep life spicy."

Sophia breathed deeply, letting their humor steady her nerves. Humor and love—they were her weapons too, almost as much as her developing powers.

Fleeting Connection

As they plotted and tested potential strategies for entering the Heavenly Realm, Sophia closed her eyes, reaching inward, hoping for even a flicker of Zephyriel's presence.

A sudden green shimmer. Just for a heartbeat, she felt him.

"I can feel you, Sophia," he said, a whisper threaded through the ether. *"I'm still here. Still fighting. Stay strong. Trust the resistance."*

Her heart tightened. "I…I won't fail you," she whispered back, and in that instant, she felt his courage, his steady determination, infusing her own resolve.

Maddie leaned over, peeking at her. "Are you talking to someone invisible again?"

"Yes," Sophia said, straight-faced. "And he just said I'm awesome."

Maddie clutched her chest dramatically. "Wow. You are officially dating someone who isn't there. Do you want me to start designing invisible matching sweaters or—"

Seradiel groaned loudly, clearly enjoying the banter despite himself. "Do not encourage her."

"Oh, I'm encouraging. Very aggressively," Maddie replied.

Training and Preparing

The day turned into hours of focused training. Sophia practiced sensing energy flows, weaving her powers through the threads of magic that pulsed across the Hollow Flame. Each time she reached into her abilities, she glimpsed potential futures: paths where she succeeded, paths where she failed, and paths where her friends or Zephyriel were in danger.

"I can feel him," she whispered again, the tiniest hint of a smile breaking through. "He's guiding me...even from there."

"You're doing more than feeling," Lysariel said. "You're learning to act, even when the threads are tangled. You're growing, Sophia. That is why we fight for you."

Maddie leaned against Seradiel, nudging him with her elbow. "You hear that? The kid's glowing, literally. And I think that makes her magicalhot. That's science."

Seradiel rolled his eyes but couldn't hide the faint grin that formed. "I said nothing. You said everything."

Sophia let out a soft laugh. Despite Zephyriel's absence, despite the Council's looming shadow, she felt alive, connected to her friends, her allies, and to the man she loved across the planes of existence.

For now, the threads between them—telepathic whispers, fleeting connections, shared visions—were all she had. But they were enough. They were enough to make a plan, to prepare, to hope.

And hope...Sophia realized...could be a weapon stronger than any angel's chains.

Chapter

23

MAPPING THE IMPOSSIBLE

The Hollow Flame pulsed with life. Not the soft, warm glow of the cathedral above, but a wild, liquid-fire luminescence of silver and gold energy, dancing along walls carved from obsidian and crystalline veins. Each flicker hummed, brushing against Sophia's senses and tangling with her nerves, sparking a thrill she could barely contain. Above the central chamber floated the celestial map, a massive, ethereal lattice of constellations and wards. Threads of sapphire traced angel patrols, while glimmers of red marked the Council's surveillance zones.

Sophia's fingers hovered over a lightly patrolled path, her hazel eyes narrowing. "If we move under the edge of this ward's shimmer, we could—"

"Get obliterated?" Maddie interrupted from the railing, legs swinging like a kid on the playground. "Or end up trapped in some divine…angel prison? Because that sounds fun. Really casual, low-stakes fun."

Seradiel's gray-blue eyes narrowed, muscles tensing beneath the golden tattoos etched across his chest and arms. "Maddie, these are not playgrounds. Each shimmer represents energy flow, patrol cycles, protective wards, and—"

"Yeah, yeah," Maddie cut in with a grin. "It's dangerous. Got it. Got it. But also shiny. And I like shiny things. Can we take it with us? Just kidding. Don't answer that."

Sophia chuckled, the tension in the room loosening slightly. Humor was a balm, even in Heaven's darkest corridors. She returned to the map, feeling the faint pulses of Zephyriel's energy, though he was trapped in the Council's prison.

A sudden warmth hit her mind—a flicker of green. Zephyriel.

"Be careful," he whispered. *"They are aware of you. Of us. Move slowly, but move. I sense something... shifting. A Council member suspects already. The threads are tightening."*

Her pulse quickened. "I know," she murmured. "I can feel it."

The wards sapped her energy even in small doses, making each mental connection exhausting—but necessary. Every whisper, every flicker reminded her of why she had to succeed.

Seradiel's deep voice cut through her focus. "Sophia, your aura is flaring. If you burn too brightly, even here, the wards could detect you."

"I'm fine," she said, though a thrill ran along her spine. "I can control it. I think."

Maddie squinted at the map. "Wait...so all these little glowing lines are like...traffic lanes for angels? And if we screw up, it's like hitting a celestial semi at seventy miles per hour?"

"Do not encourage her," Seradiel muttered, though a trace of amusement tugged at the corner of his mouth.

"Too late," Maddie chirped. "She's already imagining it. Angels honking at each other. 'Excuse me, your halo is in my lane!'"

Sophia shook her head, smiling. Maddie's humor was a lifeline.

The map shifted subtly in response to Sophia's focus, rotating and rippling as if alive. "Here," she said, tracing a path with her glowing fingers. "We follow this line through the southeast quadrant. Patrols are sparse, wards weak. Timing is everything. We stabilize the wards as we pass, or risk tripping alarms."

"Stabilize? Like...not explode?" Maddie asked.

"Exactly," Seradiel muttered. "Not explode."

Beyond the map, Lysariel—slender with silver tattoos that curled like water over his arms—gestured at a holographic diagram of the Heavenly Gates. "These wards are ancient, predating even the most senior Council members. They respond to intent as much as energy. To pass, you must anchor a conduit to the mortal plane."

Sophia inhaled, letting the knowledge sink in. "I can create the anchor...and Maddie can...keep me sane."

"Affirmative," Maddie said, saluting. "If anyone loses their mind, I'll provide commentary."

Seradiel allowed a rare smirk. "Commentary only. Nothing more."

Hours passed with Sophia studying maps, connecting briefly to Zephyriel, and practicing the stabilization techniques. Her fingertips tingled as she manipulated the wards' subtle energies. Each shift, each thread, whispered secrets of Heaven's flow. She felt herself growing stronger—and more terrified.

By mid-afternoon, Lysariel suggested a break. Sophia, Maddie, Seradiel, and a few others gathered for a rare moment of levity: a team dinner. Maddie had insisted on ordering food from the mortal realm, bringing a chaotic slice of human culture to the celestial sanctum.

"Behold," Maddie announced, setting a small platter of burgers and fries on a floating table. "Heavenly cuisine...for humans, and today, angels too."

Seradiel raised an eyebrow. "This is...edible for you?"

Sophia laughed, cutting a fry and offering it to him. "Try it. It's... different. But it keeps morale up. We need every advantage."

Reluctantly, Seradiel took a bite. His brow furrowed as the unfamiliar flavors hit him. "Salty...and greasy."

"And delicious!" Maddie exclaimed, shoving another fry toward him. "Come on, everyone has to try it. Consider it cultural diplomacy."

Lysariel hesitated, then tentatively nibbled a fry, his eyes widening. "Interesting. The textures...unusual. But I think I like it."

Sophia grinned, watching her team laugh, tasting life in small bites amid the shadow of rebellion. Even Seradiel, grumbling, couldn't hide a faint twitch of amusement. The simple, mundane act of sharing a meal grounded them all—and reminded them why they fought.

After dinner, the maps resumed their silent dance in the Hollow Flame, each thread of light a possible pathway, each shimmer a heartbeat of the Heavenly Realm. Sophia, Arion, and Lysera had already been feeding intelligence from their positions above, while Seradiel and Lysariel coordinated reinforcement schedules. Even Maddie, with her sharp quips and relentless curiosity, found her place as morale officer—and accidental ward destabilizer.

Floating above the main map alone, Sophia reached out to Zephyriel again. "I feel the paths, the pulses...we're close," she whispered.

"Faster," his voice pressed against her mind. *"They sense movement. They are watching. Each second matters."*

"I know," she breathed, fingers brushing a faint glimmer of green in the map. "I won't fail you."

"Maddie...keep her alive," he added, teasing under the tension. *"She's...dangerous. But necessary."*

Sophia smiled, the warmth of the connection anchoring her nerves. *"Noted. Dangerous and alive. I'll deliver."*

Above them, the wards shimmered in response to every thought, every pulse, every whisper of defiance. Heaven itself seemed to hold its breath. And somewhere in the shadows, the Council began to sense the stirrings of rebellion—the impossible plotted, the spark of chaos beginning to ignite.

The Hollow Flame thrummed with anticipation. Sophia floated slightly above the map, but she wasn't the only one riding the pulse of energy.

Maddie leaned against the railing, tapping her chin thoughtfully. "You know what this place needs?" she asked.

Seradiel's sharp gaze flicked toward her. "Another human interruption? I highly doubt—"

"Competition!" Maddie interrupted, grinning. "A celestial games day. Winner gets...hmm...chocolate and wine. Because if you're gonna train to outsmart angels and dodge ancient wards, you deserve treats at the end."

Lysariel tilted his head, silver tattoos glimmering like liquid starlight. "You...want to turn the Hollow Flame into a playground?"

"Yes!" Maddie threw her arms wide. "We're already in the middle of life-or-death planning. Might as well burn off some stress with a little friendly rivalry. Come on, it's practically mortal tradition."

Seradiel groaned, running a hand through his white locks. "I do not have time for frivolity."

"Sure you do," Sophia said, suppressing a laugh. "I think we all could use a break. Even you, serious golden-armored brooding type."

The angels hesitated, then slowly began forming into teams. The rules were simple: a series of challenges designed to test agility, perception, ward manipulation, and celestial coordination. Maddie volunteered as the game master, naturally.

"Round one," Maddie announced, pointing to a holographic floating track shimmering with golden light. "Ward dodging! Whoever can navigate the ward obstacle course without triggering alarms wins!"

Sophia floated forward, feeling the wards pulse beneath her fingers. Each shimmer was a heartbeat, each line a vein of energy. Moving through them required perfect timing—and creativity. Zephyriel's whispers tickled her mind, giving her hints: *"To slip past the sentinel thread, curve like a comet, don't rush, don't hesitate."*

Seradiel, predictably, surged through the course with a controlled grace that left everyone else struggling to keep up. Lysariel's silver tattoos shimmered as he weaved through with fluid motion, like water flowing through crystal channels. Maddie, of course, took a "creative" approach, bouncing off walls, shouting commentary at every shimmer, and somehow triggering only a minor shimmer alert that fizzled harmlessly.

Sophia's pulse quickened. She moved like a dance through the ward lines, feeling each energy thread brush past her aura, almost tickling. By the end, Seradiel crossed first, Lysariel second, and Maddie... somewhere in the middle, laughing hysterically.

Round two was perception: spotting minor ward distortions hidden among the larger celestial energy flows.

"This one's my specialty," Lysariel said smugly. His eyes glimmered silver as he pointed out weak spots, and Seradiel grunted, a flicker of amusement in his expression.

Maddie squinted, then shouted, "Found it! Found it! Wait...that's my snack from earlier..."

Sophia laughed so hard she almost forgot the wards beneath her feet. "Focus, Maddie! Or I'll anchor you to a mortal plane just for fun."

The final round combined agility and ward manipulation: each participant had to stabilize a miniature ward conduit while balancing on a floating obelisk of obsidian. The moment Sophia touched the first ward, it shimmered, golden sparks flying as if testing her resolve. She laughed aloud. *This is insane*, she thought—but exhilarating.

Maddie bounced from obelisk to obelisk, arms flailing, somehow managing to anchor the wards with chaotic precision. Lysariel floated with serene elegance, stabilizing everything flawlessly. Seradiel, of course, looked like he was moving in slow motion, but every pulse of his golden aura kept the mini-wards steady.

Finally, Maddie clambered up to Sophia's level, panting. "So… winner gets chocolate and wine?" she asked, wide-eyed, as if it were a sacred celestial law.

"Agreed," Sophia said, laughing. "But…let's be honest. Everyone's a winner, just because no one exploded."

"Speak for yourself," Seradiel muttered, though a faint curve at his lips betrayed his amusement.

Maddie bounced in place, crowning herself with a leaf of celestial energy she'd "stolen" from the map. "I am the champion! Bring me chocolate and wine, mortal-style celebrations for an angel-defying mortal! I demand it!"

Even Lysariel chuckled. "This…strangely boosts morale," he admitted. "I see why mortals create games and prizes. The spirit of camaraderie—even in rebellion—is vital."

Sophia felt her chest warm, watching her team revel in the chaos and laughter.

Zephyriel's voice flitted through her mind. *"Good. Keep them alive. Let them feel joy…it will matter when darkness falls."*

"And after this," Maddie added, "we need to train for real again. But first—dessert!" She held a fry like a scepter. "All hail Queen of Ward Chaos!"

Even Seradiel rolled his eyes, but when Maddie offered him a fry, he took it with a reluctant smile.

The Hollow Flame echoed with laughter, hums of wards, and the faint shimmer of celestial energy—proof that even in a place built for order, chaos and joy could carve their mark.

And somewhere deep in the map's threads, faint sparks of prophecy flickered. Angels moving, wards pulsing, the impossible plotted. But for now…for a brief shining moment…the Hollow Flame was theirs.

The laughter and clamor of the training games had barely died down when Sophia noticed something unusual on the floating map. Maddie had been swinging on the railing like a human pendulum—half-accident, half-performance art—when she had leaned too close to one of the wards.

"Whoa! Did anyone else just see that shimmer?" Maddie asked, pointing to a barely-visible line on the map that pulsed faintly in violet. "It's like a secret highway nobody told us about!"

Seradiel's gray-blue eyes narrowed, his posture stiffening. "That… should not be visible. That's a restricted zone. Impossible to access without alerting the Council."

Lysariel floated closer, eyes scanning the line with intensity. "I…I think it's a hidden conduit," he murmured. "Ancient, predating even some of the oldest wards we've studied. The Council has kept it off all standard maps—erased it from records. Only a few high-ranking members know its existence."

Sophia's pulse quickened. "Wait…so if it's hidden, it's…unguarded? Maybe lightly patrolled?"

"Yes," Lysariel said, silver tattoos flaring as he traced the line with a finger. "But accessing it incorrectly could trigger a catastrophic feedback in the surrounding wards. It's a delicate path, but it could…bypass the main defenses entirely."

Maddie's eyes sparkled like she'd just discovered buried treasure. "Ohhh, secret hidden paths! This is exactly like mortal adventure games! We should totally take it! Imagine sneaking past the Council like rogue little sprites."

Seradiel groaned. "Maddie, this is not a game. Do not treat it as—"

"Wait, Seradiel," Sophia interrupted, her mind racing. "Look at the timing of the pulses. It's…it's almost like a rhythm. We could synchronize our entry to their patrols. If we anchor ourselves to the wards we've been practicing on…we could slip in without raising alarms."

Lysariel nodded, eyes wide. "It's risky, yes, but ingenious. Only someone with...your unique connection could manipulate the anchor points without detection." He glanced at Sophia with a faint smile. "And someone like Maddie could...unintentionally provide necessary chaos to cover the approach."

Maddie puffed out her chest proudly. "I accept that role. Chaos is my specialty. I've trained for this my whole mortal life!"

Seradiel crossed his arms, clearly torn between exasperation and admiration. "I cannot believe I'm saying this...but yes. That conduit... it is our best chance. If you miscalculate, you will be...erased. But if you succeed..." His voice softened slightly, almost uncharacteristically. "You could change everything."

Sophia floated above the map, tracing the hidden path with her fingers. Each pulse and shimmer responded to her touch, as if the map itself was alive, waiting for her to make the first move.

This could work, she thought. *It's dangerous, but it's possible. And it's perfect.*

She turned to the group, her long curly brown hair catching the flickering silver-gold light.

"This is it. This is the plan for the infiltration. We train, we synchronize, and when the time comes...we enter through this hidden conduit. We stay in the shadows, and we strike when they least expect it."

Maddie clapped her hands together, nearly toppling off the railing again. "Secret tunnels! Sneaking past the big scary Council! And chocolate and wine afterward if we survive! This is my favorite rebellion day ever!"

Even Seradiel allowed a faint smirk. "I still dislike the theatrics, but...I admit, this is clever. Dangerous, but clever."

Lysariel's silver eyes glimmered with approval. "The hidden path was forgotten for a reason...but sometimes, the forgotten ways are the strongest. You are wise to notice it."

Sophia's heart pounded with a mixture of fear, excitement, and exhilaration. *This is it. This is how we'll reach Zephyriel.* She glanced at Maddie, who winked and waved a fry like a wand. *Of course, she would celebrate like that.*

"All right," Sophia said, straightening her shoulders. "We've got our path. We've got our training. Now...we make sure we survive long enough to use it."

The Hollow Flame hummed around them, silver and gold energy flowing like living veins through the walls. Laughter, strategy, and excitement mingled with the pulsing wards. Somewhere in the hidden lines of the celestial map, a path waited—forgotten, unseen, and ready to carry them into the heart of the impossible.

The rebellion had a plan. And now, thanks to Maddie's chaotic brilliance and Sophia's instinct, it had a secret path forward.

Chapter

24

SECRETS, ALLIANCES, AND THE ARMOR OF DAWN

The Hollow Flame shimmered with energy as Sophia, Maddie, Seradiel, Lysariel, and the rest of the resistance gathered around the hidden conduit on the celestial map. It pulsed faintly, like a heartbeat, responding to the presence of angels and humans alike.

"All right," Sophia said, adjusting her gauntlets and letting her hazel eyes trace the shimmering path, "we know the route. Now we need to practice moving along it without alerting the wards or the Council patrols. Timing is everything."

Maddie bounced on the balls of her feet. "Timing! I love timing. It's like mortal dance competitions…except with divine consequences. Also, chocolate at the end, right?"

Seradiel's expression remained stone, but his tone betrayed faint amusement. "Yes, if you survive. Focus on not being erased first."

Lysariel raised a hand, his silver tattoos rippling like liquid metal. "The wards are ancient. They respond to intent, to focus. You cannot simply run through. You must flow with their rhythm, almost…like a dance. Sophia, you will lead. Maddie, your chaos will serve as the unpredictable element to distract ward sensors."

"Ah, so I'm the star of the show." Maddie grinned, spinning dramatically. "I accept this role with honor!"

Sophia shook her head, smiling despite herself. "Just try not to accidentally collapse the conduit."

The first exercise began as Lysariel and Seradiel created small ward pulses along the hidden path, forcing the team to weave between flashes of golden and violet light. Sophia led, feeling the subtle vibrations of each ward as though she could hear them whispering, telling her when it was safe to move.

"Think of it like...cosmic hopscotch," Maddie said, hopping over a flash of light that nearly zapped her. "Except if you miss, you get... erased."

"You mean spiritually vaporized," Seradiel corrected, but there was a ghost of a smile tugging at his lips.

Sophia moved through the conduit with growing confidence, her long, curly brown hair flowing behind her like a banner, her athletic frame navigating each pulse with grace. Maddie followed, chaos in motion, dodging and improvising, making every misstep part of a pattern the wards could not predict.

"This is actually kind of fun," Sophia admitted, letting herself laugh as they navigated a particularly tricky sequence. "Like...extreme celestial parkour!"

As the team ran through the exercises, Lysariel narrated, weaving celestial lore into every move. "These wards were crafted during the Age of Ascension, when angels first swore to protect the mortal plane. They are alive, almost sentient. They can sense deception, fear, and even... stubbornness. Maddie, you may be the greatest test yet."

"Stubborn? Me?" Maddie feigned shock, placing a hand over her chest. "Never!"

Seradiel rolled his eyes but allowed a chuckle. Even Maddie's chaos had a grounding effect on the tense training environment.

After a few hours of ward-dodging, pulse-timing, and the occasional near-miss with divine energy, Sophia decided it was time to raise the stakes.

"Competition time," she announced. "Whoever navigates the conduit the fastest, cleanest, and without...getting zapped gets...wine and chocolate. Human wine. Dark chocolate. The works."

Maddie squealed. "Yes! Finally, stakes I can understand!"

Seradiel crossed his arms, unamused. "I will win. Efficiency is not a game."

Lysariel smirked. "Do not underestimate the human element. Chaos can be…surprisingly effective."

The team took turns moving along the conduit, each sequence more difficult than the last. Sophia felt herself pushing harder, balancing focus with speed, her body moving like a well-oiled machine honed by both human determination and angelic power. Maddie, of course, added flair, cartwheeling and spinning, forcing the wards to adapt in ways no angel had intended.

By the end, Maddie somehow managed to cross the finish line first, narrowly beating Seradiel, who had taken a straighter, more methodical route. Sophia crossed with grace, earning praise from Lysariel for her control and subtle manipulation of the wards.

"Victory is mine!" Maddie proclaimed, holding an imaginary trophy. "Now…chocolate. And wine. I demand it!"

"Focus, Maddie," Sophia said, laughing. "You'll get your reward… after we survive the real thing."

Then, as the group began to reset for another round, something on the map caught Sophia's eye. A faint glimmer in the distance—a hidden ward they had not noticed before. Maddie had tripped over a control point, sending a pulse through the map that revealed a series of previously invisible lines.

Seradiel's eyes widened. "That… should not be visible. You've triggered a concealed layer of the Council's surveillance. That ward is ancient, part of a monitoring network they do not discuss. Only the highest-ranking members know it exists."

Sophia's pulse quickened. "So…it's a secret? But it's…here? And we can see it?"

Lysariel floated closer, tracing the new lines with a delicate hand. "Yes. The Council hid this from all lower angels, even most resistance cells. It monitors movement between the high sanctums. But the conduit intersects with it…carefully, we could use this to our advantage. It is risky—but it could provide a clean entry point directly into Zephyriel's location."

Maddie's eyes gleamed with excitement. "See? My chaos always has a purpose! I knew those somersaults would pay off!"

Seradiel exhaled slowly, a rare expression of approval crossing his face. "You may have inadvertently done something useful for once."

Sophia traced the newly revealed path with her fingers, feeling the pulse of hidden energy.

"This is it. When the time comes…this is how we'll get in. Through the secret monitoring ward. We'll move like shadows, silent, precise, and unseen. And we'll take him out before the Council even realizes it's happening."

The Hollow Flame pulsed around them, brighter, alive with excitement and purpose. The training had been fun, chaotic, and exhausting—but it had uncovered the key to the impossible.

The team looked at each other, smiles wide, exhaustion tempered by adrenaline. They were ready.

"Tomorrow," Sophia said, her voice steady, "we push further. We synchronize. We perfect this conduit. And we don't just train—we prepare to change Heaven forever."

And somewhere in the depths of the celestial map, a hidden path waited, pulsing with ancient energy, ready to carry them into the storm.

Sophia, Maddie, Seradiel, and the other angels gathered around the glowing celestial map, still catching their breath.

"All right," Sophia said, tracing her fingers over the lines the wards had revealed, "now that we know the secret path…we need allies. Angels who will actually help us, without alerting the Council."

Maddie leaned against a crystal railing, arms crossed, smirking. "Oh, so basically like hosting a dinner party…if the guests could vaporize you with a look and the appetizers had swords."

Seradiel's lips twitched, a faint acknowledgment of humor. "Your strategic insight is…unparalleled, Maddie."

"Thank you, thank you," she said with a dramatic bow. "I accept this honor on behalf of chaos and sarcasm everywhere."

Sophia's eyes flicked back to the map. Threads of faint light connected to pockets of sympathetic angels—those quietly dissatisfied with the Council. "We'll approach them slowly, carefully. Every step must be untraceable. One wrong move and"—she hesitated, then sighed—"well, we could die. Or worse."

Seradiel, leaning against a pillar, gave a rare nod. "No room for mistakes. But if anyone can lead this…it's you."

Sophia's chest tightened. She thought of Zephyriel, trapped in the Heavenly Realm, counting on them. The pressure was immense, yet she welcomed it.

"Then we move with precision. Quiet, secret, together."

Maddie nudged her shoulder. "Also, jokes. Mandatory. If things start going sideways, I'm the emergency comic relief."

Sophia smiled, warmth threading through the tension. "Fine. I'll allow it…within reason."

Recruiting allies in the angelic realm wasn't just dangerous—it was unprecedented. No human had ever entered these circles, and any misstep could cause madness or death.

Sophia, Maddie, and Seradiel huddled with Lysariel and a few other resistance angels—each with a unique aura and skill.

"We need angels sympathetic to our cause," Sophia explained, spreading her hands over the glowing map. "We can't just storm the Council. We need a coalition. Secret, careful, and untraceable."

Maddie raised an eyebrow. "Oh, so basically like throwing a party, but everyone has swords and magic powers, and one wrong dance move and we're toast?"

"Exactly," Seradiel said dryly, though a faint smirk appeared. "You have a remarkable grasp on strategy, Maddie."

Maddie winked. "Thanks, I try."

The hours stretched into days. Telepathic messages from Zephyriel flickered in and out, brief sparks of encouragement.

"Move slowly," he whispered once. *"But I sense…hope. Don't let them scare you. Your instincts are stronger than theirs."*

In the quieter moments, Maddie found herself drawn to Seradiel in ways Sophia had begun to notice. The bickering, the teasing, the shared laughter—it wasn't love yet, but it was building.

Maddie leaned against him one evening, muttering under her breath, "You're not allowed to be that hot and competent at the same time. It's confusing."

Seradiel, unmoved but clearly entertained, simply said, "I am whatever the mission requires. That includes confusing you."

The Hollow Flame became a hive of whispered discussions, experimentation, and secret planning. Sophia's powers had grown stronger. She could sense patrols, detect weak points, and even glimpse short glimpses of possible outcomes in the Heavenly Realm.

Sophia stood in the heart of the Hollow Flame, the silver-gold light reflecting off her curly hair, making it shine like a dark river under the moon. She brushed a loose strand behind her ear and ran her fingers over the edge of the celestial map again, tracing a path with more confidence than before. She was playful, teasing herself aloud as she muttered, "If this works, I'm basically a celestial spy...minus the actual invisibility. I guess that's next on the checklist."

Maddie, lounging on a crystal railing, snorted. "You're basically a spy, Soph. And also the most beautiful, terrifying, and occasionally overdramatic spy I've ever met. Which is saying something."

Sophia laughed, a sound that seemed to make the Hollow Flame itself flicker with warmth. "Overdramatic? Moi? Never."

Seradiel, leaning against one of the glowing pillars, folded his massive arms across his chest. Golden tattoos shimmered across his skin, muscles flexing as he studied her. "Playful, but focused. I like that. It keeps you alive."

Sophia turned her gaze on him, hazel eyes sparkling with a teasing glint. "I can be deadly serious too, you know. I have layers, Seradiel. Complexity. Mystery. Occasional chaos."

Maddie rolled her eyes dramatically. "And yet somehow still convinced you're just an angel's sidekick."

The group's laughter faded as Lysariel stepped forward, holding a small, intricately carved chest.

"Sophia," he said in his flowing, melodic tone, "before you enter the Heavenly Realm, you must be equipped properly. What you face is beyond anything you have encountered before."

Sophia's heart fluttered. Her hands tingled with anticipation. "What is it?" she asked, leaning forward.

With a flourish, Lysariel opened the chest. Inside lay the *Armor of Dawn*, forged in the flames of Heaven itself, each piece shimmering with gold, silver, and pearl. Light danced across the surface like living fire, yet the armor radiated a soothing warmth when touched.

Seradiel stepped closer, his voice low and reverent. "It will hide you, Sophia. Shield you from detection. Protect you from the wards and the energy that would kill a normal mortal instantly. Only someone of your power can wear it without breaking it."

Maddie leaned over, peering at the armor. "Ooh, shiny! Do you think it comes in sequins? Asking for a friend."

Sophia chuckled, brushing a strand of hair over her shoulder. "I think gold, silver, and pearl will do for now. Sequins can wait until after we rescue Zephyriel."

As she lifted the armor from the chest, she felt the weight of its power. It was alive, in a way she hadn't felt before. Each piece seemed to hum with energy, almost recognizing her. She held the breastplate against her chest, feeling the warmth seep into her, and for a fleeting moment, she imagined herself standing tall before the Council, radiant and unbreakable.

Lysariel stepped closer. "You must remember, Sophia, this armor will amplify your gifts. But it will also make you visible to any angel who can sense celestial energy. You must use it wisely."

Sophia nodded, slipping into the armor piece by piece. Gold and silver kissed her skin, pearl highlights catching the light and weaving with her dark hair. When fully suited, she felt like a creature of myth—a blend of mortal beauty and divine power. Her reflection in the crystal walls seemed to radiate strength, yet the familiar warmth of her playful personality remained, shining from her eyes and smile.

Maddie clapped her hands, nearly toppling over in excitement. "Okay, wow. Soph, you're basically a goddess now. Can you promise to not use your powers to prank me constantly?"

Sophia laughed, a melodious sound that made even Seradiel's stern features soften. "No promises, Maddie. But I'll try to keep it within reason."

With their spirits lifted, Lysariel began to outline the plan. "We will enter the Heavenly Realm through the Veil of Whispered Echoes. Only a select few angels know the path, and it must remain hidden. We have allies within Heaven already—angels sympathetic to your cause—but caution is paramount."

Sophia absorbed every detail, her mind racing. Her powers had grown dramatically in recent weeks, her visions of the future sharpening. She could see glimpses of what might happen, decisions she could make that would protect her friends and the resistance—or put them in danger. Each vision, fleeting and chaotic, strengthened her resolve.

Maddie leaned against Seradiel, nudging him with an elbow. "So, what you're saying is, Sophia's about to play spy, hero, and general all at once. And we're the comic relief?"

Seradiel's gray-blue eyes softened, a smirk playing on his lips. "You may provide the comic relief, but do not underestimate your usefulness."

Sophia smiled, taking a deep breath. "Then we'll do this together. Me, Maddie, all of you. We'll bring Zephyriel back. And I'll make sure we all survive in the process."

Her hands glowed faintly as her power swirled around her, reacting to the Armor of Dawn. For a brief moment, she imagined Zephyriel seeing her like this—radiant, powerful, untouchable, yet undeniably herself. Her chest tightened with longing. Even miles apart, even trapped in Heaven, she felt their bond pulse like a lifeline.

Lysariel's voice broke her reverie. "The first step is to map the entry points, mark patrol schedules, and prepare your minds for the wards. The armor will shield you, but only your power and cunning can see you through."

Sophia nodded, her heart pounding with determination. "Then let's begin. I've waited long enough to see Zephyriel again. And I'm not waiting any longer."

Maddie grinned. "Finally, some action. I thought we were just gonna sit around talking about shiny maps forever."

Seradiel's gaze lingered on Sophia, a mixture of admiration and concern in his eyes. "The Council does not forgive lightly. And neither do some angels. Be ready."

Sophia's lips curved into a determined smile. "Then we'll make sure they regret ever underestimating us."

The Hollow Flame pulsed around them as the resistance gathered closer, every angel aligned behind her. And in that moment, Sophia

Breaking the Eternal Veil

felt a surge of power and confidence unlike anything before. They were ready to make the impossible plan a reality—and nothing, not even the Council, could stop them from trying.

Seradiel's voice cut through the warmth of the Hollow Flame, calm but edged with urgency. "I've received word. There is a small group within Heaven...angels who quietly resist the Council. They could be valuable allies."

Sophia straightened, heart skipping. "Allies? Really?"

"Yes," Seradiel continued, his eyes darkening thoughtfully. "Their leaders are Lysera and Arion. From what I've learned, Lysera is cunning, precise...a strategist whose mind rivals even the Council's. Arion is... bold, passionate, and unafraid to bend the rules. Together, they're dangerous—to the Council and anyone who stands in their way."

Maddie leaned closer to Sophia, whispering with a grin, "So we're about to meet some secret rebel angels. This just keeps getting better."

Sophia allowed herself a small, hopeful smile. The Armor of Dawn gleamed against her chest, the Hollow Flame flickering as if in agreement. "Then we'll need every ounce of wit, courage, and cunning we have," she said softly. "Lysera and Arion...I hope you're ready for us."

Seradiel's expression softened slightly, a rare glimmer of pride in his eyes. "You will meet them soon. And when you do...understand this: Not all in Heaven are loyal to the Council. Some fight quietly, waiting for the right moment."

The air hummed with possibility, and for the first time, Sophia felt a flicker of exhilaration among the nerves. Allies in Heaven, a hidden conduit, a mission that could change everything, and a friend reminding her that courage was not the absence of fear, but acting despite it.

Maddie nudged her again, teasing. "Ready to charm some rebel angels?"

Sophia laughed softly, feeling the weight of the Armor of Dawn and the pulse of her own determination. "Let's give them a reason to remember our names."

And with that, the Hollow Flame seemed to burn just a little brighter, as if acknowledging the path ahead—and the allies yet to come.

Chapter

25

SHACKLES OF HEAVEN

The battlefield was silent, except for the faint hum of residual celestial energy that lingered like smoke in the air. Zephyriel's green eyes, once blazing with defiance, now flickered with exhaustion. The clash with the Council had been brutal—angels loyal to the old ways versus angels who had questioned, hesitated, or refused. Zephyriel had fought with every ounce of strength he possessed, his sword a blur of gold and light, cutting through attackers who would have struck Sophia down without hesitation.

But in the end…it hadn't been enough.

Before he could react, a beam of cold, crystalline energy struck him from behind, knocking him off his feet. He tumbled, face scraping against the marble floor, his sword skittering out of reach. His captors were relentless, a coordinated strike from angels he once counted as neutral, but now had obeyed the Council's orders without question.

"No!" he roared, springing to his feet, fists glowing with divine energy. He unleashed a pulse, knocking two of the angels backward, but more came, circling him like predators. His muscles tensed, every fiber ready to fight, but chains of pure celestial iron shot from the ground, wrapping around his wrists and ankles in a shimmer of divine fire that burned his skin—not physically, but deep in his spirit.

The chains bit into his power, sapping his energy, dampening the glow of his wings, and dulling the edge of his abilities. He struggled, muscles straining, green eyes blazing with fury. "You'll regret this!" he spat, voice echoing in the high, vaulted chamber.

"Quiet, Zephyriel," Eryon's voice cut like ice through the air. The Council's enforcer, standing tall and impossibly regal, radiated authority and contempt. "Your rebellion ends here. Your human…accomplice is no longer your concern. You will serve your punishment, and Heaven will be restored."

Zephyriel's chest heaved. The Council had won this battle, but not the war. Not yet. He was thrown into the detention wing of Heaven's prison—a place that had claimed countless angels who'd dared defy orders. The doors slammed behind him with a finality that vibrated through his bones.

Chains clinked as he was dragged across the smooth, cold marble floors. The room they threw him into was small, barely enough to stretch his wings. The walls shimmered with wards and runes designed to suppress divine energy, glowing faintly red in warning. He fell to the ground, knees hitting the floor first, and felt the chains bite deeper.

Hours—or was it days?—blurred together. Zephyriel's body ached, but his mind refused to break. He tested the chains, each link radiating a force designed to hold even the most powerful of angels. He had been beaten, yes, but not broken. He could feel the Council's intentions through the wards: They meant to crush him, to use his absence from the mortal realm to turn Sophia against the very idea of rebellion.

The first night was the hardest. Hunger was irrelevant. Pain was secondary. What gnawed at him was separation from Sophia—the thought of her training, planning, and fighting without him and the faint echo of her laugh in his mind, carried by their telepathic bond. Even when their fleeting mental whispers broke through, it was like a knife: He felt her closeness and her warmth, then it vanished, leaving him with the cold emptiness of his cage.

He tried to move, to summon even a flicker of his power—but the wards responded violently. A shock ran through him, singeing the edges of his consciousness. He collapsed to the floor, green eyes narrowing.

"I will not stay here. I will not yield," he whispered to the empty cell.

Time dragged. Shadows of the other prisoners passed silently through the halls—a warning of what could happen to those who resisted too long. Whispers of despair and madness clung to the air like a thick fog. Zephyriel kept his mind razor-sharp, focusing on strategy, counting the ways he could escape, ways he could still reach Sophia, even if only through their shared visions.

He stretched his chains, testing every movement, every possible weakness. He remembered the subtle changes he had noticed in the Council's patrols, the moments where angels hesitated, and the loyalists within the heavenly guard whose eyes lingered too long on him. Seeds of rebellion. Allies. He filed these details in the corner of his mind. Every plan needed time, patience, and precision.

And as the night wore on, with pain radiating through his arms and the echo of Sophia's voice teasing at the edge of his consciousness, Zephyriel clenched his jaw.

They had taken his freedom. They had chained his body. They had even beaten his spirit.

But they had not yet taken his will.

And when the time came, he would rise from this prison stronger, sharper, and ready to strike back—not just for himself, but for Sophia, for their love, and for the angels who dared to defy the old laws.

Even in chains, his green eyes burned with unyielding fire.

Chapter

26

SHADOWS IN THE CAGE

The day had no name. The concept of time had become meaningless in the confines of the Council's prison. Zephyriel's muscles screamed from the chains, his wings cramped in the narrow cell. The wards continued to pulse with oppressive energy, sapping his power, dulling his divine senses. Each strike of the Council's torment left him more bruised, more battered, but his mind remained unbroken.

"You will tell us the names of those who oppose the Council," one of the interrogators hissed, voice like a sharpened blade.

Another angel, clad in robes of frost and flame, brought the whip down with precision, leaving trails of searing pain across Zephyriel's chest and arms. Every lash was meant to break him—not just physically, but spiritually.

Zephyriel gritted his teeth, green eyes blazing with defiance. The wards limited his power, but his mind remained free. He let the pain flow through him, learning its rhythm, storing it like fuel for the fire he knew would come.

"You will yield," the angel said, voice cold, almost disappointed. "Your defiance is…unbecoming."

Zephyriel spat blood onto the floor. "You can break my body. You can try to break my mind. But my will…you will never touch my will."

Hours—or maybe days—passed before the guards finally left him alone. The cell was silent, except for the faint hum of the wards. He collapsed against the wall, chains rattling, bruises throbbed, and his chest heaved with exhaustion. But even as darkness pressed in, he noticed a subtle shift—an almost imperceptible vibration in the air near the cell door.

A shadow moved.

Zephyriel tensed, expecting another Council enforcer. But the figure paused just outside his cell, barely visible in the dim light. The faintest smile touched the angel's lips.

"Zephyriel," the figure whispered.

The voice was calm, familiar in a way that grounded him amidst the chaos. Green eyes narrowed. "Who are you?"

The angel stepped closer, revealing features that shone even in the dimness. Strong, angular, with eyes that flickered a pale flame in the shadows.

"I am Arion," he said softly, his voice carrying authority and warmth. "And I'm here to make sure you survive. You are not alone."

Zephyriel's heart surged. Allies were rare, especially in this place. He studied Arion carefully—this angel had not been sent by the Council. His presence carried subtle wards of protection, and he moved with a grace that hinted at considerable power.

"I've brought food," Arion said, placing a small pouch near Zephyriel's hands. "Not much, but enough to keep your strength. Eat."

Zephyriel hesitated for only a moment before ripping the pouch open. Inside were small, glowing orbs of sustenance, infused with light. As he ate, he felt warmth return to his body, the faint stirring of power suppressed but not gone.

"Why?" Zephyriel asked between bites, suspicion mixed with gratitude. "Why risk yourself?"

Arion smiled faintly. "Because there are those of us who remember why Heaven was meant to protect, not punish. You are not a criminal. The Council is wrong. And if you fall now…everything you and Sophia have worked for will be lost."

Zephyriel's jaw tightened. He knew she was planning, training, and moving on the mortal plane; but the reality of being powerless in the Council's grasp made his stomach knot.

"I need to hold on," he whispered. "For her, for our cause, for the angels who believe in what's right."

Arion's flaming eyes softened. "Then hold on. But know this, patience is your weapon now. The Council underestimates you. And you underestimate yourself."

That night, with Arion's discreet guidance, Zephyriel tested the limits of his chains. Each movement, each flex, became a study. The iron was divine, yes, but he noted the faint weaknesses, the slight inconsistencies in the wards, the patterns in the guards' patrols. His green eyes flickered with quiet determination.

"You'll not break me," he murmured to the darkened cell. "And I'll make sure you pay for every ounce of suffering you've forced me to endure."

As sleep came—fitful, fragmented—Zephyriel's mind wandered to Sophia. Their bond pulsed faintly in his mind, brief and fragile. Even across realms, he could feel her determination, her laughter, her beauty, her fire. She was planning. She was moving. And she would come for him.

He clenched his fists. Tomorrow would bring more pain. Tomorrow would bring more tests. But he was ready.

Because he had to be.

Zephyriel sat on the cold stone floor, the chains biting into his wrists and ankles. The torchlight flickered against the walls of his prison cell, casting long, quivering shadows that seemed almost alive. His body ached from the Council's interrogations. Every muscle burned from exhaustion, and yet his green eyes—still fierce despite the fatigue—tracked every sound beyond the iron-barred door.

It had been three days since the last "session." They had thrown him into the cell without food or water, leaving him to contemplate the humiliation of his capture. The Council believed that breaking him physically would also crush his spirit. But Zephyriel had faced centuries of duty, and centuries of watching over humans and angels alike. He had endured worse.

Then a faint whisper of movement near the doorway made him tense. From the shadows, a figure emerged, careful and quiet.

"Food," the figure murmured.

A tray clinked softly as it was set down.

Zephyriel's gaze softened fractionally as he recognized the visitor. "Arion," he said, voice low. Relief and caution intermingled in his tone.

Arion, however, was no gentle courier. He was a tall, broad-shouldered angel with an aura that radiated authority and quiet power. Golden hair framed his chiseled face; and his amber eyes flickered with intelligence, determination, and something fiercer still—a quiet defiance that the Council had learned not to underestimate. His armor was lighter than the Council's standard, more functional, built for mobility, and marked subtly with sigils of allegiance.

"I didn't risk this lightly," Arion said, his voice low, but with an undercurrent of humor that Zephyriel would have rolled his eyes at in any other circumstance. "If they catch me sneaking in here, I'll have to... well, let's just say, their interrogation methods will become *my* problem. And I like my shoulders unbroken, thank you."

Zephyriel allowed a small smirk to touch his lips. "You always did like to make a dramatic entrance."

Arion crouched slightly, eyes scanning the shadows. "Dramatic? No. Strategic? Absolutely." Then with a wink, he added, "I suppose a bit of flair doesn't hurt either."

The smirk became genuine laughter. Even here, even chained and beaten, Zephyriel felt the weight of despair lift slightly. Arion was a spark—a reminder that not all of Heaven's angels were blind to love, loyalty, and justice.

"Lysera?" Zephyriel asked, immediately noting the absence of her typical glow.

"She's..." Arion's jaw tightened. "Busy. Strategizing. You know how she gets." His voice softened a fraction. "But she believes in this. She believes in *you*."

Arion had always been methodical, precise, and fiercely loyal; but what Zephyriel hadn't fully appreciated until now was how fiercely Arion's heart guided his mind. He wasn't just a soldier of the resistance—he was a thinker, a planner, someone who saw beyond the immediate fight to the *bigger picture*. And he was willing to put himself in harm's way for it.

"You've brought me food. That's...kind of dangerous," Zephyriel said, breaking the silence that had grown as they both stared into the flickering shadows.

"I've learned a few things about risk," Arion replied, a shadow of a grin tugging at the corner of his mouth. "And you, my friend, are worth every risk."

Zephyriel's gaze softened. "I'm...glad you're here."

Arion's eyes gleamed, and for the first time since his capture, Zephyriel felt a thread of hope that wasn't just a fleeting dream.

"I'm here," Arion said, voice firm now. "And we're going to make sure they regret what they did."

That night, as the other angels of the Council slept—or perhaps plotted—the first seeds of rebellion began to take root. Arion whispered strategies in the shadows, recounting every secret he had gleaned from sympathetic angels, noting the weaknesses in the prison warding spells and the patterns of the guards. He moved with purpose, but also with patience, ensuring that Zephyriel understood that this wasn't just brute force—it was planning, precision, and timing.

"You can't just storm the Council," Arion said, pacing. "Even if you could, you'd fall into every trap they've prepared. But you *can* turn their own systems against them. And if we do it right..." He trailed off, a spark of cunning in his amber eyes.

Zephyriel's green eyes narrowed, calculating. "And the others?"

"They're on board. Slowly. Carefully. But we're building more than a revolt—we're building a movement. You're not alone, Zeph. You won't be."

For the first time in days, Zephyriel felt a flicker of real optimism. Even as the chains cut into his wrists and the Council's torches flickered beyond the walls, he knew the fight wasn't just about survival—it was about reshaping Heaven itself. And with Arion by his side, he might just have a chance.

Arion lingered a moment longer, placing a hand briefly on Zephyriel's shoulder. "Rest. You'll need your strength for what's coming. And when it comes, I want you ready—not broken."

As the torchlight dimmed and Arion disappeared back into the shadows, Zephyriel closed his eyes, letting the chains dig into his skin. Pain was temporary. Hope was permanent. And the fire of rebellion had just begun to burn.

Chapter

27

SPARKS IN THE SHADOWS

The cell was quiet, but Zephyriel's mind was anything but. The first light of the celestial dawn barely filtered through the cracks of his prison, and already, he was moving, flexing against chains, testing the divine iron and wards once again. Pain still laced through his muscles, but where once he had flinched, now he calculated. Every nerve, every bruise, every pulse of the warding energy—it was all a map. And in a map, every crack was an opportunity.

Arion appeared again at the edge of the cell, eyes glinting with quiet amusement. "Still practicing," he said, voice barely above a whisper, but enough to make Zephyriel grin despite the fatigue.

"You don't get tired?" Zephyriel asked. "How are you always here?"

Arion's lips curved into a small, knowing smile. "I have…assistance."

From the shadow behind him, another figure emerged: tall, graceful, with eyes like molten violet and hair tied in a cascading braid of dark and gold strands. She moved with the fluid elegance of one born for flight, but her presence carried strength, authority, and warmth.

"And I am Lysera," she said, stepping forward, a gentle, yet unmistakable force in the dim light. "Arion told me about you. About what they're doing. About what you've endured."

Zephyriel studied her carefully. There was power here, yes, but more than that—a sense of purpose, unwavering. And in the curve of her smile, he saw hope. "I…I don't understand. You're helping me?"

Lysera's voice softened. "Yes. Because we understand the truth of love." She glanced at Arion, and the affection between them was palpable, silent but absolute. "Because love is never wrong. And if love can't exist in this place, then we will make it exist by protecting it, by protecting you, by protecting Sophia."

The words struck Zephyriel deeper than any lash from the Council ever could. Love…yes. That was his anchor. His defiance. His connection to Sophia wasn't just emotional—it was a beacon; and these two, Arion and Lysera, had become fellow guardians of that beacon.

"First," Arion said, crouching low beside the chains, "we have to understand the routines of the guards. The Council may control the physical space, but they are arrogant. They leave patterns, weaknesses. We've watched them for moons now."

Zephyriel's mind ignited. He began speaking in rapid, precise terms, detailing the guards' patrols he had noticed, the brief moments when the wards flickered, the minor inconsistencies in the divine iron. Arion nodded, taking mental notes, while Lysera placed her hand lightly on Zephyriel's arm, imbuing warmth and reassurance into the chains that otherwise seemed intent on draining him.

"You have allies here," she said softly. "Angels who see the truth, who remember that love—choice—is sacred. You need only reach out to them carefully, subtly. Fear and obedience are tools, yes, but so are courage and hope."

Zephyriel's green eyes gleamed. "I've been patient long enough. I've endured long enough. Now it's time to strike where they least expect it—and gather those who will stand with us."

Arion chuckled, a low, resonant sound. "We call them sparks. Angels who are ready to ignite, but need someone to show them the flame. That's you, Zephyriel. Even here, even in chains, you're the spark they've been waiting for."

Lysera smiled, brushing a hand through her braid. "And we'll guide you, every step of the way. Together, we can reach them, connect with the sparks before the Council realizes their hearts have begun to shift."

The trio huddled, whispering and plotting, mapping out a vision that was impossible if approached recklessly—but achievable if patience, love, and cunning were applied. Zephyriel felt the surge of his resolve, fueled by more than defiance: fueled by connection, by the knowledge that even here, even in the Council's prison, he was not alone.

Hours—or was it days?—later, Arion and Lysera left the cell, silent as shadows, leaving Zephyriel to contemplate their words. He pressed a hand against the cold stone, feeling his heartbeat echo through his chest, echoing with the promise of action.

Even through the fatigue, the pain, the bruises, he allowed himself a small, dangerous smile. He could taste it now: rebellion. The first whisper of upheaval.

And he knew, with certainty, that the Council had underestimated the power of *love*.

Zephyriel leaned against the cold stone wall of his cell, the chains now familiar weights, more a reminder than a restraint. Pain had dulled into a rhythm of endurance, and his mind sharpened in its absence of distraction. Every flicker of torchlight reminded him of the Council's rigid vigilance—and every shadow whispered possibilities.

The cell door creaked softly, and before Zephyriel could react, Arion slipped inside, light on his feet like a predator and a guardian rolled into one.

"Still in one piece," Arion said, leaning casually against the wall, his amber eyes glinting in the torchlight. "Mostly. Though I imagine the Council would like to introduce me to their 'disciplinary' methods if I lingered too long."

Zephyriel allowed himself a small smirk, despite the ache in his chest. "And you'd enjoy that?"

"Only if it came with cake," Arion replied dryly. Then more softly, he said, "I didn't come here for cake."

The words carried weight, a quiet resolve that Zephyriel had come to trust, but Arion was more than just a skilled rebel operative—he was a man shaped by love and loyalty, and now those qualities were weapons in their fight.

"You never told me about your story with Lysera." Zephyriel said, voice low, nodding toward the faint sigil on Arion's armor that symbolized a bond long and sacred.

Arion's jaw softened. He leaned forward slightly, resting both hands against the stone floor. "We've been bound together since the early days of the Celestial Concord." There was a glint of something painful in his eyes. "She believes in love, in the sacredness of choice. When the Council turned blind eyes to the injustices...she couldn't stand by. So she's helping me now, even if it puts her at risk."

Zephyriel's green eyes narrowed in understanding. "So your rebellion...this isn't just strategy. It's personal."

Arion's amber gaze softened. "Everything worth fighting for is personal, Zeph. Love is never wrong, even if the Council tries to convince us otherwise."

The moment was brief. Plans had no patience for sentiment. Arion pulled a small parchment from his armor, scrawled with celestial symbols that shifted subtly, almost alive. "I've been mapping the weak points in the Council's patrols, their warding patterns, rotation shifts. With your knowledge of Heaven's inner sanctums, we can start turning the system against them."

Zephyriel leaned closer, studying the patterns. "You've done your homework," he murmured. "I like that."

"I *am* meticulous," Arion replied, a smirk tugging at his lips. "Lysera taught me that love doesn't just make you soft—it sharpens your edges if you use it right."

Zephyriel allowed a brief laugh. Even chained, hope and camaraderie were beginning to solidify into a tangible force.

"Here's what I've discovered," Arion continued, pointing to a series of runes that glowed faintly under the torchlight. "Certain wards are tied to celestial pulses—if we can manipulate the timing, I can get you out of the cell without triggering the alarms. But..." He paused, voice dropping to a whisper. "The Council's eyes are everywhere. One wrong move and they'll make an example of us. You, me, Lysera, everyone who touches this plan."

Zephyriel's eyes flashed green with determination. "We've never been about safe moves."

Arion chuckled softly, but there was steel in his tone. "You sound just like Sophia. That girl has a fire, doesn't she? If I were you, I'd protect her like she's the last light in the heavens. She's...more than just a human girl with powers. She's a force."

Zephyriel's jaw tightened, and his fists flexed against the chains. "I intend to. But first, we free me. Then we free Sophia."

Arion's smile widened, tinged with pride. "Exactly. And you'll have more allies than you think. Lysera's network, angels like me...we're all watching, waiting for the right moment. And the right moment is coming."

He glanced at Zephyriel, amber eyes sharp. "I need you sharp too. Not just physically, but mentally. You'll have to anticipate every move, exploit every crack, and—"

"Make them regret every decision they made," Zephyriel finished, voice low and deadly.

Arion grinned. "Exactly. Now, let's review the rotation shifts again. And I'll tell you about Lysera—her own strategies are brilliant. The two of us together have started a web they'll never untangle."

For hours, they poured over the celestial maps, plans sketched in glowing ink and whispered secrets of the Council's routines. Each strategy, each contingency, strengthened their bond. And each whispered plan carried the unspoken truth: Love, loyalty, and rebellion were entwined, and the first sparks of Heaven's insurrection were beginning to ignite.

When Arion finally left, shadows swallowing him as he slipped back into the corridors, Zephyriel rested against the wall. For the first time since his capture, chains no longer felt like limitations—they were challenges. And for the first time, he believed the impossible might just be achievable: turning the Council's own rules into their undoing, guided by allies, love, and a fire that could not be extinguished.

28

WHISPERS OF REBELLION

Zephyriel sat in the dim glow of his prison cell, chains clinking softly as he flexed against them, testing the limits of divine iron yet again. The council thought him broken. They thought his spirit would bend under the weight of solitude, the ceaseless punishment, and the knowing that Sophia was beyond his reach. But the truth was far more dangerous—they had underestimated him.

Through the quiet, fleeting moments of connection with Sophia, their minds brushing across the veil, he felt her strength and determination. Her visions, growing sharper each day, now guided them in secret. And with every glimpse, he plotted, marking paths of escape and rebellion in his mind.

Yet even as Zephyriel worked, the rebellion didn't stall. Far above, in the shadows of the celestial hierarchy, Arion and Lysera moved with precision. They were the eyes and hands of the cause, gathering intelligence, mapping the guards' rotations, and quietly planting seeds of dissent among angels who had grown weary of the council's rigid laws.

Arion leaned against the edge of a balcony, arms crossed, his dark muscles flexing under the low light, golden tattoos glinting faintly. Lysera's braid swayed as she approached, her violet eyes scanning a scroll of celestial logs.

"Another patrol shift changed," Arion murmured, voice low and deliberate. "If we time it right, we can get a message to Zephyriel tomorrow through the ward shadowing. Only a small window, but it'll be enough."

Lysera raised an eyebrow. "You and your precise timing. I swear, if this was a human rebellion, you'd have already started arguing over the snacks and coffee breaks."

Arion smirked. "You know me. Efficiency over pastries any day."

Lysera laughed softly, a sound that carried warmth and resolve in equal measure. "Well, Seradiel's running into the same problem on the other side of the city. He keeps arguing with your angels over dinner logistics. Apparently, even rebels need to eat."

"Seradiel?" Arion chuckled. "The human-side recruit? That one cracks jokes at the worst moments?"

"Yes," Lysera said, rolling her eyes fondly. "He's insufferable, but funny. And loyal. Don't underestimate him."

—ॐ—

Meanwhile, across the city, Seradiel leaned against a pillar in the Hollow Flame's training courtyard, tossing an enchanted dagger into the air and catching it with precision. Maddie stood nearby, arms crossed, lips twitching in amusement.

"You know," Maddie said, smirking, "for someone who's supposed to be a golden, terrifying angel, you make juggling knives look like a circus act."

Seradiel shot her a look, one eyebrow raised. "You're laughing now, human. But you'll see the value when this rebellion succeeds."

Maddie rolled her eyes. "Oh sure, can't wait to be famous for cheering for angels while they overthrow their own council. Realistic career path."

"Not cheering," Seradiel corrected, tossing the dagger into his other hand. "Contributing. You humans underestimate how much your cleverness can help. And you've got the advantage—your kind sees patterns differently."

Maddie grinned. "Ah, so you're saying I'm essential because of my humor and sarcasm?"

Seradiel laughed softly, the sound low and rare in the tense environment. "Exactly."

—ɯ—

Back in his prison cell, Zephyriel quietly observed a flicker in the warding magic around him. That flicker—the tiniest, almost imperceptible gap—was the opening Arion and Lysera had been waiting for. Messages, subtle as whispers, now traveled through the magical currents of the celestial realm.

He received them in the fleeting telepathic moments they shared, a spark of connection that reminded him why he had to survive. With each message, he learned of which angels were leaning toward the rebellion, which were still loyal to the Council, and which were uncertain, watching silently, hearts torn between obedience and conscience.

Zephyriel leaned back against the cold stone, green eyes gleaming. Each name, each strategy, each whispered promise of loyalty strengthened his resolve. The rebellion wasn't just a plan—it was a movement, a tide that would sweep through Heaven itself, fueled by the truth that *love could not be contained*.

Lysera and Arion, meanwhile, were more than just messengers. They had begun training the sympathetic angels in secret, teaching them subtle ways to resist the Council's commands, methods of covert communication, and defensive techniques that wouldn't trigger suspicion. Every angel who joined the cause was a small victory, every minor act of defiance a spark to ignite the larger fire.

And through it all, Seradiel and Maddie served as a bridge between the human side of the rebellion and the celestial resistance. Their playful banter and undeniable camaraderie lightened the heavy burden, but also sharpened their coordination. Maddie's humor and resourcefulness complemented Seradiel's strength and celestial intuition, making them an effective pair.

"Ready for tonight's run-through?" Seradiel asked, tossing the dagger back into the air with flawless precision.

"Born ready," Maddie said, spinning a baton like a juggler in a street performance, grinning. "Let's make sure we don't accidentally blow up a hallway, yeah?"

As night fell, the Hollow Flame glimmered with unseen energy, secret whispers, and the low hum of angels preparing for what was coming. Above, in the heavenly spires, the Council remained oblivious, blind to the alliances forming beneath their noses, to the rebellion quietly taking root.

And in his prison, Zephyriel smiled. The time was coming. The time when Heaven would see that love, defiance, and courage could not be chained.

Chapter

29

SPARKS OF REBELLION

The Hollow Flame hummed with energy, the secret sanctuary beneath the cathedral alive with quiet determination. Sophia moved among the angels, her long curly brown hair catching the flickering torchlight, her hazel eyes shining with equal parts determination and mischief. Despite the gravity of the situation, she still carried herself with the playful warmth that made everyone around her feel both at ease and inspired.

"Okay," Maddie said, arms crossed, pacing in front of a celestial map spread across the floor. "So let me get this straight—we're sneaking a human into Heaven. You know, where humans aren't supposed to go because…sanity problems. That's the plan?"

Seradiel, standing nearby, arms crossed over his broad chest, golden tattoos catching the light, sighed. "Yes. And before you ask again, yes. There are ways to stabilize you, but it's not perfect. You follow Sophia's lead. Don't touch anything glowing. Don't ask questions. Just survive."

Maddie snorted. "Noted. Don't touch anything glowing. Got it. I've never been more prepared for a field trip in my life."

Sophia laughed softly, stepping closer to Seradiel and Maddie. "You two make a perfect team. Maddie keeps it real, Seradiel keeps it… terrifying. Balance." She traced a finger along a shimmering line on the celestial map. "Here. This is where the wards are weakest. If we move fast, stay hidden, and use the diversion Arion set, we can get in, rescue Zephyriel, and get out before the Council even knows what hit them."

Arion leaned against the wall, arms crossed, a wry smile on his face. "And you're sure Zephyriel can hold himself long enough? We're pushing the window here."

Sophia's jaw tightened, a flicker of frustration crossing her otherwise calm features. "He'll hold. He has to. And we'll make sure he isn't alone for long."

Maddie elbowed Seradiel, whispering with a grin, "You think he knows how cute Sophia gets when she's stressed?"

Seradiel rolled his eyes but allowed a small smile. "I think he does. And I think it annoys him."

The sound of laughter, faint but warm, carried through the sanctuary, a stark contrast to the looming danger. It was a reminder of what they were fighting for—and why.

Hours later, Sophia stood before the assembled angels of the resistance. Lysera and Arion flanked her, their faces grim, but there was a spark of excitement in their eyes. The plan was ready. The allies were briefed. The time had come to move.

Sophia felt the familiar hum in her chest, the subtle pull of Zephyriel's presence in her mind. A fleeting moment—a shimmer in the veil. A whisper of his voice: *"I'm waiting for you."*

Her pulse quickened. She closed her eyes, letting the connection ground her. *Soon,* she thought, *I'll see you again.*

Meanwhile, in the heart of the heavenly prison, Zephyriel shifted in his chains, muscles taut, green eyes burning with defiance. He had spent months subtly gathering intelligence, observing guards, noticing patterns, and sowing seeds of doubt in angels who had grown weary of the Council's rigid laws.

One by one, sympathetic angels approached him in the shadows. Some brought small comforts, others whispered promises of support. Among them was Arion, who had risked everything to bring Zephyriel news from below.

"The Council doesn't know who's truly loyal," Arion murmured, voice low. "But it won't last. They never see it coming when love and determination are on your side."

Zephyriel nodded, chest heaving. "We'll turn their rules against them. We'll show them that the bonds of love and loyalty are stronger than fear."

—⟋⟍—

In the Hollow Flame, Sophia donned the celestial armor, the golden-silver-pearl plating forged in the flames of the heavens itself. It hugged her form like a second skin, reflecting light in a soft shimmer. She adjusted the pauldrons, feeling the weight of the mission settle on her shoulders.

Maddie clapped her hands together. "Okay. Fancy armor, check. Secret human hero, check. Let's go cause chaos and maybe save a Greek-god-level angel while we're at it."

Seradiel gave her a pointed look. "Stay alive. That's your first priority. After that, do whatever you want."

Sophia smiled, adjusting her gauntlets, her heart pounding. She could feel Zephyriel's essence, faint but guiding, as if his energy wove through the very threads of the Armor of Dawn. She glanced at Maddie, who gave her a thumbs-up, and Seradiel, who nodded once. The resistance angels were ready.

And then, with a deep breath, Sophia whispered under her breath, "For Zephyriel. For Heaven. For us."

The Hollow Flame shimmered, a secret doorway appearing in the hidden depths of the cathedral, pulsing with energy. It was their passage to the impossible: the celestial plane.

As they stepped through, Maddie let out a dramatic, high-pitched whistle. "Well, this is definitely going to end with a story I can tell my grandkids…if we survive."

Seradiel muttered, "I don't even want to think about that right now."

Sophia gritted her teeth, determination radiating from her every move. Every step brought them closer to Zephyriel, closer to the moment when the rebellion would ignite in full force. The Council had no idea what was coming.

And above, unseen, the first tremors of chaos stirred in Heaven. Loyal angels whispered, guards questioned orders, and the seeds of rebellion planted by Zephyriel, Arion, Lysera, and their allies began to bloom.

The final confrontation was near. And no one—not even the Council—could foresee the storm that was about to fall.

The Hollow Flame was quiet now, but the air was thick with anticipation. Lysera and Arion huddled over a set of celestial maps, their fingers brushing as they traced the wards, noting patrols and weak points. The light from the torches caught Arion's amber eyes, sharp and calculating, and Lysera's dark hair fell over her shoulder in soft waves as she leaned closer, whispering.

"You're thinking three wards over, then a double diversion at the southeast tower?" Lysera murmured, lips curved into that half-smile that always tugged at Arion's chest.

"Exactly," he said, his hand brushing hers again, lingering longer this time. "If we misstep, Sophia won't make it past the first ward. And Zeph…" He paused, eyes hardening. "He deserves more than mistakes."

Lysera chuckled softly, squeezing his hand. "You're adorable when you're brooding over your prisoners. But, yes, I agree. Timing is everything."

Arion's lips twitched, a grin threatening to break his otherwise serious expression. "Adorable? I'll take it as a compliment." He leaned closer, eyes locking on hers. "And if this works, we get to see them all freed. I'll even let you have the first celebratory dance."

Lysera laughed, the sound like sunlight breaking through clouds in that shadowed underground sanctuary. "You know I'll hold you to that," she said, and the warmth in her tone made their shared determination feel almost effortless.

They returned to the maps, fingers pointing, tracing paths and contingencies, feeding each other intel they'd gathered from the loyal angels scattered throughout Heaven. Arion's network was vast, and Lysera's instinct and quick thinking made them a perfect team. Each whispered observation was exchanged with affectionate nudges, subtle smiles, and the quiet acknowledgment that they weren't just allies—they were life mates, bound by love and trust that even the Council couldn't break.

"Seradiel's positioning is solid," Arion said, scanning a particular warding glyph. "But he can't move too far without tipping the other patrols. We'll need a secondary diversion to draw attention away from him. Lysera, that's where your team in the lower rings comes in."

"Already in motion," Lysera replied, leaning over the edge of the table, tracing a route with her finger. "They've been planting misdirection, spreading rumors of phantom patrols. By the time the Council notices, it'll be too late. Sophia will have Zeph, and the others will secure the exits."

Arion exhaled, brushing a lock of hair from his forehead, and for a moment, his guard slipped.

"You know," he said quietly, "watching you coordinate like this… it's contagious. I think everyone else in the Hollow Flame feels it too. You make them believe they can win."

Lysera's violet-tinged eyes softened as she reached for his hand, entwining fingers with his.

"We *will* win," she said, voice steady and sure. "Because we have to. And because love doesn't fail when it counts."

The two of them sat like that for a long moment, the flickering torchlight painting their faces in gold and shadow. Their hands remained locked, the quiet intimacy of shared purpose a sharp contrast to the chaos waiting for them above. Around them, whispers of rebellion grew louder—loyal angels reporting, plans adjusting, contingencies layered like intricate threads in a tapestry only they could read.

Arion leaned closer, his voice a conspiratorial whisper. "If Sophia had any idea how much we're relying on her… she'd probably roll her eyes and tell us to stop coddling the plans."

Lysera laughed softly. "And yet, we're the ones with the advantage. She's brilliant, but she's human. She needs us just as much as we need her."

They exchanged information late into the night, trading intelligence with a precision born of love, trust, and countless hours of quiet observation. Each whisper, each nod, each hand squeeze solidified the framework for the coming storm. Even from the safety of the Hollow Flame, the rebellion was alive, pulsing with energy and intent.

And though the Council remained oblivious, Arion and Lysera knew this: Every ally Zephyriel had, every strategy Sophia devised, every careful diversion and whispered warning brought them closer to a tipping point. The storm was ready to break—and they would be the lightning that lit the skies.

Their fingers remained intertwined as they stood together, surveying the maps one final time. The Hollow Flame felt alive with hope and danger intertwined. The rebellion wasn't just a plan anymore; it was a heartbeat, a pulse running through every loyal angel, every whispered secret, every carefully laid trap.

The final confrontation wasn't just coming—it was inevitable. And in that moment, Arion pressed a gentle kiss to Lysera's temple, a silent promise amidst the chaos. She smiled, tightening her grip on his hand.

The storm was near. And when it fell, Heaven would never be the same.

Chapter

30

INTO THE VEIL

The portal from the Hollow Flame shimmered and pulsed like liquid silver as Sophia, Maddie, Seradiel, and the rest of the resistance crossed into the celestial plane. The air immediately shifted—light heavy and alive, a humming energy vibrating beneath their skin.

Sophia's heartbeat raced, her golden-silver-pearl armor warm and protective, attuned to her spiritual aura. She could feel Zephyriel nearby, a whisper of his presence flickering in her mind, fleeting but enough to ground her.

Hold on, Zeph, she thought. *We're coming.*

Maddie stumbled slightly on the shimmering floor, immediately regaining her footing with a dramatic flair. "So...wow. Heaven. Not exactly what I imagined. No clouds with unicorns? No giant harp-playing cherubs?"

Seradiel, arms crossed and expression stoic, muttered, "You might want to save the commentary for after we're alive."

"Hey, I'm helping with morale!" Maddie quipped, flipping her hair.

Sophia shot her friend a small, amused smile but kept her focus on the path forward. The celestial realm was breathtaking, but treacherous. Wards flickered and shifted with every step, a reminder that detection could mean instant annihilation. Every angelic patrol they passed radiated authority, and Sophia's heart clenched thinking of Zephyriel chained somewhere close yet unreachable.

Arion led the way, whispering directions, his eyes scanning the skies and structures of light. "This is as close as you'll get without drawing attention. Follow my lead and stay sharp. Even a misstep could bring the Council down on us faster than we can blink."

The group moved cautiously, telepathic threads keeping Sophia in constant fleeting contact with Zephyriel. A soft tug in her mind reminded her of his struggles—his pain, his strength, and the growing cracks in his chains of isolation.

"Every step we take brings us closer to him," she murmured. Her voice was soft, almost to herself, but her eyes were fire.

Maddie nudged her elbow. "I think you just talked to your boyfriend telepathically. That's… that's hot and terrifying at the same time."

Sophia's lips twitched in a rare grin. "It's not a date, Maddie. Not yet."

Seradiel snorted. "You're killing me with that restraint."

They finally reached a hidden enclave that Arion had prepared for them—a small cluster of structures shaped from clouds of condensed light, tucked behind a veil of shifting celestial energy. It was a safe haven, invisible to most angels, a place where the resistance could regroup.

Sophia exhaled, removing her gauntlets and stretching her fingers. "We're here. Temporary, but enough to plan, breathe, and—hopefully—get Zephyriel out before he weakens too much."

Maddie immediately plopped onto a soft glowing bench, flopping dramatically. "Breathe? Oh yeah, sure. I'm just gonna casually chill in the land of overpowered celestial beings while our boyfriend is—somewhere—being tortured. Totally normal."

Seradiel gave her a dry look, but Maddie didn't miss the subtle humor. "What? I have to keep it light. Otherwise, I'd cry."

Sophia's expression softened, looking at her friend with warmth. "You're strong, Maddie. Stronger than you know. And funny. That matters too."

Meanwhile, Arion and Seradiel began laying out celestial maps and markers, discussing safe routes, patrol cycles, and potential allies within Heaven.

Lysera joined via the ethereal communication link, her voice calm but tinged with urgency. "The Council is already noticing anomalies.

We have a window, but it's shrinking. Move carefully. Timing will be everything."

Sophia leaned over, tracing paths on the map. "We'll need to create distractions, signal our allies, and—most importantly—get Zephyriel out before they regroup. Every second counts."

Hours passed in strategic planning, the weight of the mission pressing on everyone. Yet, beneath the tension, moments of levity threaded through—Maddie joking about Seradiel's intense focus, Sophia teasing Arion about his obsession with celestial patrol rotations, even Seradiel allowing a rare chuckle at one of Maddie's sarcastic observations.

When the night finally settled in, Sophia found a quiet corner, her armor removed but still glowing faintly from the energy of the realm. She closed her eyes and let herself reach for Zephyriel's mind, feeling the strain of his chains, the bruises on his soul.

Hold on, Zeph. I'm coming for you.

A whisper, faint and fleeting: *"I know. I'll be ready."*

Her chest tightened. The Council's shadow loomed everywhere yet hope burned brighter in her heart. This was only the beginning of the real war.

From the other side, Seradiel leaned close to Maddie, who had sprawled across a glowing bench, making a dramatic sigh. "So, what's the plan if things go sideways?"

"Step one," Maddie said, wiggling her eyebrows, "don't die. Step two, make our enemies underestimate us because apparently, they *love* doing that." She gave Seradiel a mischievous smile. "Step three, have fun while we're at it. Heaven doesn't know what hit it."

Seradiel shook his head, a faint smile tugging at his lips. "I think I'm going to like working with you."

Sophia watched them, a small smile on her face, before returning her attention to the map. Soon, the infiltration would begin. Soon, she would see Zephyriel again—or at least try.

Above them, unseen but not unfelt, the Council stirred. Their spies reported movements, their whispers carried threats. Yet the seeds of rebellion, planted carefully by Zephyriel and his allies, had begun to bloom in silent defiance.

And at that moment, in the safe haven of Arion's home, with the Hollow Flame resistance at her side, Sophia knew one thing: The real battle was coming. And it would change everything.

The hideout pulsed with soft, shifting light, walls and furniture sculpted from condensed clouds that hummed faintly when touched. Small spires of solidified starlight jutted from the floor like crystalline trees, their surfaces reflecting the glow of the realm above. Sophia ran her fingers along one of the benches; it shimmered beneath her touch as if remembering the hands of every angel who had ever sat there.

Maddie wandered the enclave, eyes wide, lips slightly parted. "Okay, okay, this is…insane. I mean—look at this place! Glowing clouds that actually hold you, trees of pure light, and—" She tripped on a translucent step that shimmered like liquid mercury. "Oh! That was supposed to happen. Totally."

Seradiel's brow twitched. "Careful. The realm isn't just beautiful—it reacts. The wrong step, the wrong gesture, and the wards notice."

"Oh, right," Maddie said, brushing herself off. "Note to self: Stop testing Heaven's furniture like it's IKEA. Definitely should've read the Bible more…or at all, apparently."

Sophia chuckled, shaking her head. "You're going to give them a reason to track us with that commentary."

Her words were almost prophetic. A ripple of energy shimmered across the far wall—subtle, but unmistakable. Patrol. Angels of the Council.

Arion's hand shot up, fingers tracing a sigil in the air. A section of the hideout shimmered and bent, folding into itself like water folding around a stone. "Quick—shadows of the Veil. Now!" His voice was calm, yet urgent.

The group melted into the altered space, hearts hammering. The floor beneath them seemed to hum, responding to Sophia's aura, weaving protective illusions that masked their presence. Maddie pressed her face to a wall of light, whispering, "So this is what Hogwarts would look like if it had better architecture and more terrifying faculty."

Seradiel's hand on her shoulder was firm. "Silence. Every sound could give us away."

154

From outside, the Council patrol moved, their wings brushing against the ambient light. Each angel's aura radiated authority, their presence a palpable pressure that made the air shimmer with tension. Sophia could feel it in her chest—a pull, a warning, a test of her concentration.

One patrol lingered longer than it should have.

Maddie froze, eyes wide, whispering, "They're like... bigger, brighter...terrifying. And very judging. Did you know angels could glare with literal divine authority? Because now I do."

Seradiel's lips twitched, almost amused despite the danger. "Don't let them sense fear."

"Fear?" Maddie whispered. "I'm...just overwhelmed with awe. That's totally different."

Sophia's hand rested lightly on Maddie's back, grounding her. "We've got this. The Veil is strong, and our concealment is tied to the armor. Focus on your breathing."

The patrol finally drifted past, wings stirring the air with whispers of ozone and light. The group exhaled collectively, the tension dissipating but leaving adrenaline behind like sparks in their veins.

Arion relaxed slightly, his amber eyes scanning the area. "Close call. Too close. But you see why we move carefully here. Every shadow, every shimmer...could be a trap."

Maddie flopped dramatically onto one of the glowing benches again, giggling nervously. "If I make it out of here, I'm definitely reading more sacred texts. Or maybe just Googling angel etiquette."

Sophia smiled softly, brushing a loose strand of hair from her face. "You're scared, I can see it. But you're here anyway."

Maddie's smile faltered just enough to reveal her vulnerability. "Yeah...scared as hell. But I'm still here. I don't know why, but I'm here."

"That's brave," Sophia said, reaching for her hand and squeezing it gently. "Terrified, yes. But brave. That's what matters."

The enclave pulsed with quiet reassurance, light weaving around them like a protective embrace. But even as they tried to settle, a faint flicker in the air drew Sophia's gaze—a shimmer not from the Veil, but from the map projected above the table. A pattern, subtle but unmistakable, seemed to move beneath the layers of wards.

Her breath caught. "Wait...that wasn't there before."

Seradiel's eyes narrowed. "Show me."

The light revealed a hidden channel, a pathway not even the patrols seemed to acknowledge. It threaded through the clouds, behind the patrolled zones—a secret route deep within Heaven itself.

Maddie leaned over, eyes wide. "Uh...does that mean...we just found a secret passage? Like...jackpot-level secret passage?"

Sophia's fingers hovered over the glowing lines. "It's...a way in. A place we can reach Zephyriel without being detected."

Arion's expression darkened, lips pressed into a thin line. "Yes. But that knowledge comes with a cost. If the Council even suspects it exists..."

A low rumble echoed through the enclave as if Heaven itself shivered at the mention.

Maddie swallowed audibly. "Uh...guys? Did the sky just threaten us? Or am I imagining things?"

Seradiel placed a firm hand on her shoulder. "Not imagining. And that's why we move fast. This is the first real advantage we've had. But it's fragile. One misstep, one careless laugh..."

Maddie smirked nervously. "Well, then we'll just have to be careful...and hilarious at the same time. Multitasking at its finest."

Sophia's gaze lingered on the hidden route, a mix of awe, anticipation, and worry. The path was there, shimmering in silver and gold like a promise, a chance, a trap waiting for the unwary.

And then, faint but undeniable, a whisper of wings—a second patrol—swept closer, almost brushing the edge of their veil.

Sophia froze, Maddie stifled a squeak, and even Seradiel's posture stiffened.

"Now," Sophia whispered.

The enclave folded in on itself like liquid light, shadows swallowing their forms just as the patrol passed within mere feet, unaware. The hum of the realm seemed to hold its breath with them.

When the patrol finally drifted away, Maddie exhaled so loudly she almost knocked over a spire of starlight.

"Okay… if I survive this, I'm definitely writing a strongly worded Yelp review for Heaven. Ten stars, but the staff is terrifyingly efficient."

Sophia, still focused on the hidden pathway, murmured, "It's our way in. Our chance."

Arion and Seradiel exchanged a tense glance.

And above them, unseen, the Council's eyes shifted. Somewhere deep in Heaven, a ripple of unease spread through the ancient halls. The game had begun.

A single, faint voice whispered through Sophia's mind: *"They know someone is coming…"*

Maddie's hand shot out to clutch Sophia's arm. "Uh…did Zephyriel just send us a text? Because that was terrifying."

Sophia didn't answer, eyes fixed on the glowing secret path. The cliff of danger loomed ahead, but so did hope.

And Heaven waited.

Breaking the Eternal Veil ended here. The sky over Heaven trembled, the Council unaware that the tide was already turning, and the storm was only beginning to rise.

www.ingramcontent.com/pod-product-compliance
Lightning Source LLC
Chambersburg PA
CBHW020620250626
47154CB00004B/1595